No Escape
Deadly Waters
by
Michael Galitello
with
Dakota Lawson

Published by Cookie Books

This book is dedicated to all those who work in the film industry. They create the fascinating worlds we live in for a few hours at a time, as entertaining fictional escapes from real life and as imaginary realms in which we can learn the real truth.

Chapter One

"The trap is set. All we can do now is pray that this works," Kim whispered into her walkie-talkie.

She sat crouched behind a wrecked car, peeking over the top of a crushed roof. Her blonde hair was full of grime and she was covered in cuts and bruises. Her eyes were fixated on a small, slow-moving object making its way down the road towards the intersection. It resembled a dog, though it didn't have a head, and instead of a sleek coat of fur, it had a cold, bright yellow exterior with a box on its back.

It slowly trotted around the corner and Kim moved forward, careful not to make a sound, first hiding behind a roadblock, then behind a dumpster.

The machine made its way through the streets of the small Bali town and approached a crossroads packed with wooden stalls. What was normally a busy market full of people selling fresh fruits, vegetables, and fish was now an empty, desolate street.

Bananas, oranges, and other fruits lay scattered around the street. The robot stopped in its tracks next to a destroyed fish stall and paused for a moment before emitting a loud, ear-piercing siren. Kim, now hiding behind another road barrier about a block away, kept her eyes glued to the machine as it blasted its alarm.

"Does anyone have eyes? I'm making the call now. Someone please tell me if they hear it?" she pleaded into her walkie.

All she heard was static as she awaited a response.

Thud. Thud. Thud. Thud. A distant booming sound had begun, barely noticeable.

"Heads up, Kim. The bogey is headed your way," a gruff voice finally replied over the radio.

"Good." She paused for a moment, letting the information sink in.

"Right. Good. That thing is heading straight for me and that is definitely a good thing," she reaffirmed to herself before she could get a chance to think about backing out.

THUD. THUD. THUD. THUD.

The sound grew louder as the ground began to shake at each vibration. Kim slunk back down behind the barrier and sat with her back pressed against it. She tried to control her breathing as she pulled a small remote from her pocket and stared at the single, small red button on its surface. Her thumb gently gilded back and forth over the button, holding herself back from the luring temptation to smush her thumb into it and let it all be over.

THUD. THUD. BOOM. CRASH.

She could hear another market stall being destroyed. She closed her eyes as all her senses were overloaded. The sudden strong waft of the worst combination of salt water and rotting fish. The rough, uneven surface of the concrete barrier digging into her back. The agonizing siren that blared from the dog-machine. Now it was mixed with an even louder clicking sound, comparable to a dolphin's voice.

Well, if a dolphin was the size of a building, she thought. She could only wish it was a giant, friendly dolphin making its way down the street.

She forced her eyes back open and slowly turned around to peek over the side of the barrier. What she saw made her heart leap. She'd never been this close to it before. What lumbered before her only a block away was the largest, most grotesque creature that she had ever laid eyes on. It lumbered on, fifteen feet tall, with a dark red and brown exoskeleton. Eight sharp limbs protruded from the main structure of its frame, all spread out and settled on various parts of the street. One of them now sat in the middle of the newly crushed fish stall.

The creature had two more of its limbs suspended in the air. The right one was only slightly larger than its legs, though its left arm carried a significantly larger pincer that held the limp body of a dead pig.

Two stalk-like appendages emerged from the front of the main shell, topped with large, beady, black orbs. Underneath the stalks was a portion of shell that moved in sync to the loud clicking sounds it emitted. It was its mouth, and it was dripping slimy mucus.
The beast focused its beady eyes on the small robotic dog, clearly annoyed by the high-pitched screech it gave off. It released the dead pig from its iron grip and dropped it onto an abandoned car on the side of the road. The car's alarm started sounding and drew
the attention of the giant crustacean.

"Damn," Kim whispered to herself.

The creature was no longer focused on the small robot dog. It gave off an eerie screech, almost to imitate the car alarm, and reached down to pick the pig body back up off the car. It dangled the corpse in front of its face and stared at it for a few moments before shoving it into its amalgam of a mouth, chunks of meat and bone crunching and slipping through before falling to the ground.

The beast looked down at the chunks it had dropped, and quickly returned its attention to the loud robot dog. It gave out another screech mid-chew, spit chunks of meat
and slime onto the robot before it grasped it in its claw.

Kim froze. Her breath went silent. Her heart stopped in its tracks. This was it. This was the moment she'd been waiting for. She watched as the creature eyed the contraption before it gave another screech and lifted the yellow
contraption up and forced it into its mess of a mouth.

"That's it, big boy," Kim whispered. "Enjoy your last meal."

She stood up from behind the barrier, the remote held tightly in her trembling fist.

"Hey, Crabzilla!" she shouted at the beast.

The creature turned its gaze towards her, still chewing on its metal-rich snack. It lifted its legs from the rubbish they were buried in as it scurried its way over to Kim.

"Go to hell!" she screamed as she pressed the red button on the remote.

The crab erupted in a giant explosion.

"Cut!"

The studio erupted in loud applause. Tim Horton walked over to Kim, whose real name was Laura Stone, and held out his hand.

"Amazing work, Laura. You really sold it on that last scene. We should have everything we need now to start putting this film together."

Laura looked him in the eye and shook his hand.

"Thanks, Tim. So, we're done?" she asked.

Tim smiled a big, toothy grin at her through his thick beard.

"We're done!" he replied. "Now, it's time to celebrate and relax! Will I be seeing you tomorrow?"

Laura ripped the blonde wig off her head, revealing her naturally brown, short-cut
hair underneath, tied up in a small ponytail.

"Yeah, I will be there. I could use this trip."

"Excellent!" he exclaimed. "I can't wait. Now, I've got some unfinished business
with the editors. I'll see you tomorrow!"

Tim patted Laura on the back and walked off.

Laura wiped a bead of sweat off her brow and made her way to the snack table for a refreshing cup of water. A small group of actors and crew members stood there stuffing their faces and rehydrating after a long day of work. Among them, his back turned towards Laura, was an unusually scruffy man in dirty, torn up khaki shorts splattered with dark red stains. He sported a dark blue Hawaiian shirt that was torn to bits from the chest down and exactly one sandal.

Normally his appearance would make anyone do a second take. This was not the case for the actors of this studio, however, and certainly not the case for anyone who had been helping produce his next big blockbuster, Crabzilla.

"And here I thought you might have actually been eaten by a giant mutant crab," Laura said as she walked up to the man. He lazily turned around in the middle of stuffing a chocolate glazed donut into his mouth.

He swallowed and, without missing a beat, replied, "Gee, I didn't realize you held my acting skills in such high regard."

He pulled a flask out of his torn-up shorts and took a swig, washing down his donut, before putting it back in his pocket and shoving the rest of the donut into his mouth.

Laura watched in disgust, but she was used to it. She had been married to the man for the better part of twenty years, after all. His name was Nathan Stone. He had shoulder length dirty blonde hair and a scraggly 5 o'clock shadow that looked so rough you could use it to sand a block of wood.

"Flattering," she said sarcastically as she pushed him to the water cooler. "Are you going on a camping trip tomorrow?" She pulled a bottle of water out of the cooler.

"I hate camping," Nathan said while sucking the sugary glaze off his fingers. "But an all-you-can-eat, seafood cuisine, bottomless bar, all while sailing the seas of Bali for the trip to the island and on the trip back? I suppose I can deal with roughing it in the sand for a couple days." He gave her a wink, stuffed a bag of chips into his back pocket, grabbed a couple slices of pizza, and shuffled off.

Laura rolled her eyes and downed her water. She looked around the studio and watched as the rest of the cast and crew scurried about doing their jobs and socializing among themselves.

She watched Tim, the director of the production, talking to the video editors with a notepad in his hand, flipping through it at high speeds. The cinematographer, Elizabeth Napier, was among the group listening to Tim's notes and thoughts. Tim's assistant director was scrambling around the set, seemingly talking to everyone he came within a three-foot radius of. Nathan was talking to a younger actress on the set who seemed invested in their conversation. She held her smile big and bright throughout Nate's chit-chat.

"Typical," Laura whispered to herself. "Just another day at the office."

Chapter Two

The next morning Nate wandered down the docks of the Benoa port in the early hours, his backpack slung over one shoulder and a cup of coffee to-go in his hand. The sun had just barely peeked over the horizon, and it didn't help him walking that it was still rather dark out.

At the end of the floating docks, he saw a small group of people crowding around a ramp that led up onto a large luxury yacht. This was the right boat, alright, he thought. He had spent plenty of time shooting scenes on this ship over the last couple of months. As he walked past the bow of the boat, he could see the bright golden letters sprawled across the side of the hull. Sail Happy. Nate smiled.

"That's the plan," he said aloud.

He approached the group and began to make out the faces in the dim morning light. Henry Stevens stood awkwardly next to Tim, who probably forgot he was even there as he was so lost in a conversation with Laura. Although Henry was the assistant director of the movie, he was the youngest and quietest person Nate had ever come across in that position. He was a good kid, and he did his job well, but he could never seem to find a place to fit in when it came to the socializing aspects of his job.

An older man with a short, white beard came walking down the ramp that led up to the deck of the ship. He was followed by two younger guys, each wearing a uniform of navy shorts and white polo shirts. Nate grinned and made his way towards the ramp.

"…to date on the location of that storm out to the west. We should be back by the time it gets here, but much like the sea, the weather is unpredictable," the bearded man said with a gravelly voice to his crew.

"Aye, aye, Captain Sterling," Nate said as he patted the captain on the back. "Are we expecting rough waters ahead of our trip?"

Captain Sterling refocused his gaze on Nate and let out a wheezy laugh.

"Well, well, well, if it isn't Nathan Stone deciding to come back to the very ship that led him to his death. You look like you're ready to be gobbled up a second time!"

Nate laughed. In a way, that was true, he thought. His outfit didn't deviate much from what he had worn in the film. Instead of a tattered blue Hawaiian shirt, he wore a new yellow one with a crab pattern design. His ripped and stained khaki shorts were now just simple tan shorts, and he was wearing the same sandals he had on the set. He had found them to be a lot more comfortable than he had expected, although, of course, now he had on both sandals of the pair.

"Ah, but this time the tables have turned. I am ready to eat enough crab to save the
the entire island of Bali! Twice over!"

The captain let out another hearty laugh.

"Aye, well, you've come to the right place. We've got the finest cuisine prepared for our trip to the island today. I hope you're all packed up and ready to go?"

Nate shrugged his backpack further up on his shoulder.

"Got everything I'm going to need right here," he said casually. "And also right here." He pulled his flask out of his back pocket and shook it at the captain before taking a
quick swig and returning it to the safety of his pocket.

"Good man!" Captain Sterling beamed. "Now, if you'll excuse me, I have a few more things to see before we set off. But everyone is welcome to start boarding and making
themselves at home!"

He stepped off the ramp and walked down the dock, resuming his conversation with
the two crew-hands who followed close behind him.
Nate liked Captain Sterling. He was a kind man whom he had spent a lot of time with during the filming of Crabzilla. Sterling had rented out his yacht to the crew for the film and had even played a small role in exchange for their advertisement of his cruise line.

Nate walked up the ramp and set his sandaled feet on the yacht once more. He scanned the top deck and took a deep breath. His vacation had finally begun.

The morning passed by quickly. After the rest of the crew had arrived at the dock, the Sail Happy set off to embark on its lengthy voyage from Port Benoa to their remote
island destination. Everyone settled in and enjoyed the luxuries the cruise had to offer.
By noon Nate was sitting at the bar enjoying himself, taking sips out of a bright green mojito with a little yellow umbrella, all while staring out at the endless ocean surrounding the ship. On the sun deck, Laura lay out on a sun chair in her bathing suit, getting some much-needed rest and relaxation and working on her tan. In the chair next to her lay Amber Wang, the same girl who had been enthusiastically chatting up Nate in the studio the day prior. Her long black hair was sprawled out behind her across the deck chair and her eyes were covered by her round purple sunglasses. She had earbuds in and was softly
singing along to her music.

At the bow of the ship in a long red sundress Elizabeth was leaning on the railing taking photos of everything she could with her camera. The occasional humpback whale breaching the surface, the flat horizon where the pale blue sky met the dark blue ocean, the seagulls that followed the ship in hope of a free meal of crackers, fruit, or anything else they could get. She was entranced with the natural beauty she found out at sea.

At the stern of the ship was a low portion of the deck that just barely glided over the surface of the ocean. There were rails on the sides and a small ladder to help climb back onto the ship after a relaxing swim. At the top of the ladder sat Tim, his fishing rod cast out into the water. His feet were buried in the water, his jean shorts just barely touching the surface. He also wore a Hawaiian shirt, dark green and unbuttoned and revealing his hairy chest. Completing his vacation attire was a white bucket hat that sat tilted slightly over his eyes and protecting them from the sun.

Standing next to him was his assistant director, Henry Carlson, in a simple maroon bathing suit and a white t-shirt. He had a beer in his hand and was rambling on about ideas they could still work into Crabzilla. Tim wasn't paying too much attention.

The yacht intercom came to life with a familiar gruff voice.

"Attention, all partygoers. If you're hungry, head on over to the main deck for our seafood buffet. I'm having it carted out as we speak so don't miss out on the delicious dishes we have prepared for you!"

One by one the film crew made their way to the dining area on the main deck. Nate, who was sitting on a stool at the bar, leaned backward and watched as the yacht hands pushed large silver carts full of plates of gourmet food into the center of the dining area. He let out a whistle.

"Damn," he said. "Looks like Captain Sterling really went all out for us today."

Tim walked over to Nate at the bar and also eyed the food as it rolled by. Laura and Elizabeth sat down at one of the tables and Henry and Amber settled down at another.

After the platters of food were set out, the crew hands left and Captain Sterling walked down the steps from the bridge deck where he'd been standing.

"Ladies and gentlemen…and Nate…lunch has been served!" He said with a smile
and a bow.

They walked over and gathered around the spread and started loading their plates with shrimp cocktail, calamari, veggie kebabs, fried clams, lobster tails, Cajun boil, and, of course, plenty of crab. There were crab cakes, crab legs, crab Rangoon, crab gumbo, and more. If there was a known dish with crab in it, it was there.

When they others had cleaned the last of the food from their plates, Nate stood
from his seat and held up his drink, now a rum and coke.

"Here, here!" he exclaimed, his words now slightly slurred. "I propose a toast to Captain Sterling! For, without him, we wouldn't have been able to make the masterpiece that will be Crabzilla."

Everyone raised their glasses to his toast and cheered before taking their sips.

"And to the Sail Happy," Nate continued, his glass already half empty, "the only
beautiful ship worthy of withstanding our crab beastie itself!"

Captain Sterling let out a laugh and said, "Here's hoping!" He took another sip of his own glass of rum before walking to the center of the deck. "In all seriousness, however, I would like to take a moment to say a few things. I wanted to thank you all, especially Mr. Horton, for giving me this opportunity to be a part of your production. I served in the Navy for the better part of thirty years and have been retired for the last six living in Bali and running my tour business. At first, I told myself it was to keep myself financially afloat…"

"Ha!" Nate let out a laugh before taking another sip of his drink.

Captain Sterling continued, fighting a smile at his own dumb joke. "…no pun intended of course. However, my business has provided me not only financial wealth, but wealth of the soul, too. But it wasn't until Mr. Horton approached me with this opportunity and we started filming that I finally realized that. I hadn't been ready to give up my life on the open sea after I retired, and I knew that deep down when I started this business. So, know that I mean it when I say that I am very grateful to all of you for making me part of this project. Not only was I able to boost the recognition of my Bali Sea tours, and reawaken my passion for the sea, but I had the honor of spending time with every one of you and I must say, it truly was a pleasure."

He raised his glass amid the applause from the cast and the lingering yacht hands and finished off his rum and set his glass down on a table.

"Now, if you'll excuse me, this ship is not going to navigate itself. I must return to my station, and I will let you all know when we have arrived at the island."

Captain Sterling left the dining area and made his way back up to the bridge and the helm of the ship where his first-mate, Gage Cooper, sat in the captain's chair in front of a panel of controls.

"I'll take it from here, Mr. Cooper," Captain Sterling said as he entered the cockpit.

Gage got up and swirled the chair so the captain could take his place in it.

"I kept her steady, sir. The seas are still calm so it should be smooth sailing for the
remainder of the trip."

Sterling sat and flipped a couple of switches to his right and the ship radio came to life. Static hissed into the room, with an occasional, nearly unintelligible conversation between other ships. The only words

Sterling and Gage could make out were "sunset," "waters," and "fajitas," although that last Sterling wasn't sure he heard correctly.
He started fumbling with the radio knobs, adjusting the frequency and hoping for a
more clear transmission.

"Damn this lousy radio. Remind me to get someone to fix this when we get back to the port… ah! There we go."

The radio finally landed on one clear transmission coming through.

"Bzzz…approaching from the east, right now passing through the northeastern tip of Australia. So far it looks like it's heading south-southwest, so be advised, anyone heading out or on their way to Port Hedland, Aussie. As it stands, it appears to be a category one cyclone, with the potential to grow into a category two. All sea craft northwest of Australia and south of Indonesia be advised. Repeat: at the time of this recording, Friday the 11th, March, 2022, at approximately 15:35, a tropical storm has been spotted approaching from the east, right now passing through th…bzzz"

Static cut off the transmission as Sterling continued trying to adjust the radio knob.
"Still have a storm brewing down there it sounds…" he muttered, half to himself, half to Gage. He glanced at his first mate, who had been staring out the window to the east, almost as if searching for something. "Don't worry. We won't be getting any of that action while we're out here. If we do see any of that storm, it will just be on our way back home."

Sterling was still fiddling with the radio knob when a different voice slipped through the static.

"Hello out there, this is the Sea Breeze. Anyone in the area? My position is negative ten degrees, 47 minutes and
one-point-seven-eight-zero-two seconds by 109 degrees, 34 minutes and

14-point-five-two-three seconds, south of Cilacap and east of Christmas Island. Does anybody copy it?"

Sterling's eyebrows furrowed in curiosity as he picked up the microphone and
brought it to his mouth before pausing briefly and staring out the window.

"This is Captain Sterling of the Sail Happy, I hear you loud and clear Sea Breeze. Everything alright out there? Are you in trouble?"

He waited for a response as Gage walked over closer to listen to the conversation.
Nothing for 5 seconds, 10 seconds, 30 seconds… then the voice returned.

"Greetings, Captain Sterling! This is Captain Ronan. We are smooth sailing on this side, just wanted to give anyone nearby a heads up. We encountered a shiver about 15 minutes ago, looked like they might have gotten a couple of dolphin calves from a local pod…" and the voice cut short again.

"What's a… shiver?" Gage asked.

Captain Sterling held up his index finger as if to say "hold on."

The voice on the radio resumed.

"…in a frenzy. It's been a while since I've seen them act like this. I don't know if you were around for the 'engagement' of
twenty-eighteen?"

Captain Sterling's eyes squinted as if in reminiscence as he spoke. "Aye," he started, paused, and then continued, "I remember the engagement. We'll keep our eyes out. Thank you for the heads up, Captain Ronan."

"No problem, Captain. Be safe out there."

Silence filled the air in the cabin. Gage stared at the captain, looked out the window, down to the radio, and then back at the captain.

"Uh, sir? What was that all about?" he asked.

Captain Sterling kept his eyes on the horizon, silent.

"What's an engagement? Is it serious?" Gage asked, speaking a little louder in hopes of an answer.

Sterling breathed a deep sigh, but remained silent while he considered his words.

"Hopefully," he finally started, "something we will not have to worry about. But I suppose being my first mate, you have every right to know. Especially if you're going to be sailing these waters on your own one day. Take a seat, Gage."

Gage hesitated before sitting down on the narrow cushioned couch behind the
captain's chair.

"So…" Sterling began, one hand on the wheel, the other brushing along his beard and rubbing his chin. "I was only two years into my retirement when the engagement of twenty-eighteen occurred. God, it was a bloodbath…"

Chapter Three

That evening, as the sun began its descent towards the horizon, Laura sat in her sun chair, still digesting the massive mixed meal of lobster and other crustaceans. A couple chairs down from her was Nate, passed out on a chaise lounge, his arms sprawled out and hanging over either side of the chair. a little umbrella hanging out of his mouth. *Honestly*, Laura thought, *I'm shocked he had even made it to dinner.*

On the other side of the deck, Tim was leaning against the railing around the top deck of the boat. He had a bucket tucked underneath his left arm.

"Got your safety bucket?" Laura called out to him, teasingly.

He turned and looked around, as surprised, as if he were snapped out of a trance. He saw her and smiled back.

"Naw," he replied and reached into the bucket and pulled out a lobster tail before
turning back and tossing it out into the ocean.

"Come on over. Come check this out!"

He beckoned to her, and Laura, intrigued, stood up and made her way to his side and peered into the bucket to confirm that, yes, he had a bucket of lobster tails, wads of fish meat, and other scraps presumably left over from the buffet. She recoiled from the smell that suddenly wafted up from the bucket. It had smelled a lot better earlier when it was fresh and still on the table. Now, not so much.

"Tim, what are you doing with a bucket of fish...?" She stopped herself when she looked out into the water. Next to them, riding the waves in sync with the yacht, was a dolphin. It bounced happily above the water right alongside them, almost as if trying to get the attention of the ship itself.

Tim reached back into the bucket, grabbed a nice juicy fish head, and tossed it. The dolphin leaped out without missing a beat and grabbed the head out of the air before
disappearing back into the crystal blue.

"Beautiful creature, isn't it?" Tim murmured, still staring into the water.

Before long the two of them saw the dolphin gliding under the water and catching
back up with the ship.

"She's gorgeous…" Laura said, almost in a whisper. She, too, had fallen into the
trance that had captivated Tim only moments before.

Suddenly a voice croaked over the intercom system.

"Attention! Guests of the Sail Happy. We are approaching our destination and should arrive in about an hour. I would advise you all to get your things together in the next few minutes so we can have a smooth departure to the island and get you guys set up before dusk."

"That sounded like the first mate. I wonder where Sterling is," Laura said. She didn't let his absence bother her too much as she was still watching the dolphin, now leaping the waves again right beside them.

"Well, I suppose we should go and get ready," Tim said and started to tear himself away from the endless sea that sprawled out before him. He waved to his newfound aquatic friend. "I have to get my pole and tackle packed up, too. See you in a bit?" He dumped the rest of the fish scraps and guts overboard.

"Sure," Laura responded, "I should get back into warmer clothes, anyways. It's
starting to get a bit chilly."

At the rear of the ship, Captain Sterling stood atop the small lookout tower, a spyglass in his hand. He gazed across the horizon, checking out the formations of the clouds and the condition of the waves. He stared out to sea as the sun slowly made its descent, turning the sky into a warm shade of orange.

As he scanned the waters, he noticed a gentle commotion disturbing the rhythmic waves a couple hundred yards off the stern. He raised his spyglass to his eye to get a closer look, and when he finally focused the lens, his hair stood up on the back of his neck. He pulled away his spyglass, stared at the spot, then looked through it once again, as if he couldn't believe what he was seeing.

"Blimey." he muttered under his breath. "You best not get any closer. There's
nothing here for you."

Sterling grabbed his walkie-talkie. "Eric," he barked into it. "Start getting the dinghies packed up, I want them ready for departure as soon as we reach the island." As he kept his focus on the movements that broke the waves out in front of him, he
heard Eric's voice break through the brief silence.

"Sure thing, Captain. Is everything alright?"

"Everything is fine," Sterling responded, as if he were trying to reassure himself. "I

I just want to get them set up before it gets dark, so the sooner they're ready, the better."

Sterling took one last look out at the sea and then climbed down the little tower and made his way back to the helm of the ship. Gage was there, once again manning the
controls.

“I’ll take it from here, Gage. I need you to help Eric load up the dinghies.” Gage glanced at the Captain, who had already taken hold of the wheel.

“You got it, Captain. I don’t suppose you saw a whole bunch of sharks out there,
did’ja?” he asked, jokingly.

The focused look on the captain’s face and his lack of a response told Gage that it
It was time to take things seriously.

Gage hurried out of the cabin and found Eric, the second-mate, by the starboard railing of the ship. Suspended over the side of the boat were two dinghies being loaded with an assortment of supplies including coolers filled with various meats and vegetables for grilling and a portable travel-grill for camping. Eric was in the process of tucking a large first-aid kit into a side pocket of the first dinghy when he noticed Gage.

“Hey, man, can you help me with the kitchen-box? It’d really save me some back problems later on.”

Gage nodded and grabbed one side of the box. It wasn’t too heavy, especially for the two of them, but it was a bulky crate that was way too large and awkward for one man to carry on his own without hurting himself.

They heaved the box up onto the second dinghy and strapped it snugly into the back. Then they piled the tents, sleeping bags, cots and umbrellas onto the two dinghies until both boats had just enough space for a couple of passengers each.

“There, all packed up and ready to go.” Eric said, trying to hide his slightly heavy breathing. “Hopefully nothing falls off on the way to the island. I don’t know why Sterling couldn’t wait for us to stop and set anchor to pack these up. It sure would have been easier with him and Mateo helping us."

Gage looked out toward the horizon, trying to see… something. Did the captain's intense look back at the helm just now have something to do with the warning they had
heard over the radio or the story Captain Sterling had told him afterwards?

"I don't know," he replied to Eric, also now watching the waters. "But he seemed pretty concerned when I saw him. We're probably better off just trusting him and following his orders." He glanced back at Eric, now starting over at him quizzically. "Besides, the sooner we set these guys up on the island, the sooner we can get back to the ship tonight and get some sleep. I'm beat."

Eric broke into a smile and held out his fist.

"Amen to that, brother. Looking after these rich Hollywood-types really takes a toll on you. They make taking care of the regular tourists seem like taking care of a bunch of fake plants."

Gage laughed as he reciprocated Eric's gesture with his own fist-bump, and together

They walked back to the cabin to get their next orders.

* * *

Nathan stood at the railing on the side of the ship, staring out at the bright blue sky without a cloud in sight. The sea was calm, almost still. He felt at ease, but then he felt the ship lunge forward following a loud crunch.

"Hey, Captain! Are we hitting some turbulence today or what?" he called out to nobody in particular. There was no one else on deck and he heard no response from the
helm above him.

Nate looked around, grinning, and he realized that the boat had stopped moving. There was no sea foam splashing up the sides of the ship anymore. Heck, he thought, the
the boat doesn't even seem to be rocking. It was completely still.

Everything remained quiet until a soft, easy to miss sound broke the silence as if someone had just broken the surface of the water after a refreshing swim. He looked over
the side into the water, but saw nothing.

He turned around to look across the rear deck only to come face to face with a single meaty looking stalk rising over the other railing of the yacht. Nate froze in shock.
Where was everyone else? What was this large antennae looking thing and…why does it look so familiar?

A fleshy flap unfolded itself at the top of the stalk to reveal a bulbous black orb, darkly eerie, and looking straight at Nate.

"Um… hello!" Nate finally said it.

Almost immediately his world was thrown into chaos. The ship lurched hard onto its side and something big came crashing up through the ocean surface, drenching the deck in slippery saltwater.

Nate righted himself and looked back at the stalk only to see a giant, ugly, old acquaintance. Towering before the yacht was no other than the giant beast he had known to be…

"Crabzilla."

The moment the name left his lips, the ship churned again, this time toward the giant crustacean. Both of its claws had latched on to the side of the yacht and it pulled it closer to its hungry, slimy mouth pincers.

Nate held onto the railing in horror as the ship tilted further into the water. He
knew what was next. Crabzilla was about to have a seafood buffet of its own.

Nate looked up at the giant crab and saw it open its mouth, but it wasn't getting ready to take a giant bite. Instead, thousands of smaller crabs crawled out of its gaping oral cavity and stormed the ship, covering every inch with salty sea-smelling red and orange shells. They began piling on top of each other, forming a bridge for the rest of the crabs still spewing from the crustaceans mouth to reach Nate.

"No!" he screamed.

He pulled himself up and dove over the railing, only to find a dark thunderous storm throwing waves fifty feet into the air. The ship had lost control.
Two dolphins leapfrogged the waves out in the distance in front of Nate. He
wouldn't have noticed them if it hadn't been for the large shapes mounted on top of each.
Nate squinted. The shapes were Laura and Tim.

"Tim!" Nate shouted, but the storm was so loud he couldn't even hear his own
voice. "Get off my dolphin, Tim!"

Suddenly, Crabzilla emerged from the ocean and swallowed both Tim and Laura whole. A second huge Crabzilla shot out of the ocean next to the first. Then, one by one,
more came up to the surface.

Nate tried swimming away from the yacht through the rough waters, but the first crab quickly caught him in a vice-like grip, nearly crushing his ribcage, and brought him up to its face as if to inspect his next tasty treat.

Looking down at Nate's tiny face, it spoke in a soft, almost soothing voice.

"Nathan," it said. "Nathan, it's time to go."

Nate, too panicked to think things through, struggled and thrashed around in the
claws of his predator.

"No! I won't go with you! You can't make me! Let go!" Nathan woke up with a start.

He was on the yacht. Everything was quiet. He felt a panging headache ripple across his brain.

"Hey, sleepy," said a soft voice.

Nate looked down at his shoulder and found a hand resting on it. He looked up and
saw Amber with a big smile on her face.

"You were really out for a while there, buddy. Come on. We're heading to the island. Go grab your stuff and I'll save you a seat on the next boat!"

Amber walked off toward the other side of the ship to depart for the island, leaving Nate lying on his chaise lounge and rubbing his puffy eyes, trying to process reality once
again.

Nate finally stood and made his way unsteadily toward the dinghies that he remembered had been hung over the side of the ship. One of them had already left for the island. In the other sat Laura, Tim, and Amber. Gage was getting the lines ready to lower the boat into the water. Seeing Nate, Amber smiled up at him and patted the seat next to her, inviting him to sit.

Nate climbed in and sat down.

"It's a bit cramped in here, isn't it?" he joked.

"Trust me," Gage told him. "You're better off on this boat than the first one. That one had to carry your two cohorts and their baggage, two of the yacht crew, and the coolers of food and totes of supplies."

Gage started lowering the boat into the soft, rippling waves below. Nate pictured Elizabeth and Henry for a moment buried under the pile of supplies in the other boat and
smiled.

"So, what were you dreaming about?" Amber asked him. Nate was still nursing his humorous visualization of Elizabeth and Henry.

"What?" he asked.

"Before I woke you up, you were mumbling something about the captain and crabs in your sleep. Did that seafood buffet give you some fishy dreams?"

Nate didn't have a response to that, but he was briefly put off by the idea that she
wasn't necessarily wrong. That was an intense fishy dream alright, he thought to himself.

"I don't really remember," he lied. He pulled his flask out of his pocket and took a
swig.

Laura rolled her eyes at him. "Shocker," she said sarcastically. Nate winked at her.

Gage climbed down and sat at the back of the dinghy and started the engine. The
machines whirred to life, and they set off toward the island.

It wasn't a very large island. It looked to Nate more like a sandbar than anything. There were six tall palm trees lumbering in the center of the island and a few large shrubs dotted the sandy surface of the little strip of land. One of the trees hung in a curve over a flat area of the beach where the first boat had already landed and the thick foliage of its palms cast a large yet fading shadow over the site as the sun sank beneath the horizon..

The others were unloading the equipment onto what would be their campsite. Eric and Henry stacked coolers and crates on top of each other while the third mate of the crew, Andrew, stuck tiki torches into a semicircle of spots in the sand. He lit them as he went along to provide a new source of light for the camp as dusk set in.

Elizabeth stood off by herself further down the beach, scanning the scenery and
taking photographs.

The second dinghy made landfall and Eric and Andrew cheered at their arrival.

"They made it! Ladies and gentlemen, welcome to paradise!" Eric yelled out.

Gage cut the engine and hopped out, pulling a rope up from the floor of the dingy. He began tying it up to the other dinghy, which had already been anchored to the
overhanging tree. Everyone climbed out, stretched, and began removing their things.

Nate stumbled as he stepped out, but Amber grabbed his arm and helped him regain his balance. Tim slung his large, metal frame hiking backpack over his shoulder and walked down the beach to Elizabeth.

"Taking any good pictures?" he asked. "Did you already set up your stuff? Everyone else is unpacking…"

She ignored his hinting at her unhelpfulness with the camp prep.

"I've been working for the last year. I am in vacation mode right now. Besides, I have a one-person tent. It takes five minutes to set up." She said to him without breaking her gaze at the horizon through the camera lens.

Tim shrugged. She was right. This was their vacation after all. He glanced around
and watched Henry and the crew unloading gear from the dinghy.

"Henry over there must have missed the 'vacation' part of the memo. Look at him trying to figure out what to do with all that stuff." Tim chuckled as he watched in
amusement.

"That's because he knocked an entire cooler of shrimp and salmon overboard on our way over to the island," Elizabeth said. "I think this is his way of trying to make up for it." Tim looked at her, surprised, and then looked back at Henry.

"Not the salmon, Henry!" he called over, taunting him.

Henry looked up and his face reddened in embarrassment.

"I'm sorry, guys." Henry called out, still trying hard to be helpful to the ship crew. "That's okay!" Amber yelled at him from where she sat in the sand. "I don't really like salmon, anyways. As long as there is still some lobster for tonight." She smiled and winked at Henry, but his face reddened even more.

Tim laughed at the scene and turned back to Elizabeth, who still was paying no
attention to anything but her photography.

"Alright. Hey, Elizabeth. Will you send me some of those when we get back?" He
asked.

"Mhmm, sure" she affirmed.

Tim found a spot in the sand and started setting up his tent, a simple and classic style canvas shelter that had seen many areas of the world. Tim was no stranger to the outdoors.

As he staked it into the sand, he watched everyone else setting up their own spots.

In the encroaching dusk Elizabeth had begun setting up her solo tent, and she had been right, Tim thought. It was a quick set-up. Amber and Henry were starting to work on their tents, as was Laura, who had a large tent that was almost family sized. She appeared to be struggling with it.

Tim scanned around the beach to see where Nate had gone off to and why he wasn't helping his wife set up the tent, and he spotted a bit of white cloth poking out from behind the overhanging tree. He set his things down and circled over to it and found a white hammock tied up between two trees with a still body lounging inside of it. It was Nate, and from the looks of things, he was already out.

Tim chuckled to himself, admiring Nate's ability to set up camp while hungover and do it efficiently. He was a little jealous, even. It made him wonder why he hadn't brought a hammock, too.

He walked back over to the campsite and finished staking his tent down. Laura was still working on her tent, but at this point she was just struggling with the rain cover. Everytime she got one corner hooked on, the opposite corner would snap out of place.

"Hey! Can I offer you a second set of hands to help with that?" Tim asked as he
walked over.

Laura looked up and just stared at him for several seconds. She wasn't sure if she should accept or reject his help. She hated the idea that she, a woman, looked too weak or dumb to put a tent together, and needed the help of a strong masculine figure. She knew the only reason the rain cover wasn't staying on was because two of the cloth loops that anchored the cover to the tent had snapped, forcing her to find other ways of attaching the hooks to the tent.

At this point, though, she decided she was too tired to keep trying to deal with it on her own.

"Yeah," she said. "I'm trying to get the cover on, but the loops broke. I have to find just the right place to hook the cover on, but it just keeps flying off."

She felt she had gotten across to him that the complications were from the tent itself and not because she's incompetent. Still, he seemed like a nice guy.

Tim grabbed the opposite corner and studied the loops briefly.

"Oh, yeah. I've had to deal with this little song and dance before, too. Hold on. I've got just the thing."

He walked back to his tent and crawled inside. After some shuffling around, he came back out, walked up to her and handed her one of two objects in his hand, a rubber band that looked to Laura suspiciously like its previous location had been on a red crustacean.

"Believe it or not," Tim began, "I did not get these from lunch on the boat. I have a small baggies of these I take with me when I go camping."

He knelt down at the corner of her tent and looped the thick rubber band around the bottom corner of the tent, twisting it, and hooking the rain cover to it. He tested the
strength, and it stayed in place.

Laura began doing the same thing on her side. Tim stepped back and watched.

Laura was impressed at his resourcefulness but not wanting to show it.

"You're telling me you didn't swipe these from the yacht?" she asked, a good natured smile on her face.

"Naw," he shot back. "The ones I swiped from the yacht I used to hang my lamp up inside my tent and to hold my fishing pole together while it's disassembled."

Laura looked up at him, smiling more broadly. He smiled back and winked before he walked back to his tent.

Back on the yacht Captain Sterling was doing his rounds to make sure everything was properly prepared for a night anchored off the island. He made sure the equipment that didn't need to be running was off, the lines were all properly secured, and everything else that he normally had his crew take care of. Though it was nearly dark now, he kept glancing out at the sea expecting to see… something.

Finally he pulled out his walkie-talkie and radioed Gage.

"Captain to Gage. Don't take too long out there tonight, alright? I still might need a hand with a few things when you guys get back."

He waited.

"You got it, boss," a voice responded back through the radio, followed by a thud
and the sound of disturbed, rippling water.

Sterling was about to respond when it clicked in his brain that the thudding and
water sounds had not come through the radio.

He heard another thud. This time he knew it was coming from the rear of the yacht. He pressed the walkie-talkie button.

"Thanks, Gage. Everything in the cabin is all set for the night, and I checked most of the lines. I'm going to go check the back of the boat. We may be parked right over a rock or something. I think I can hear it scraping against the hull of the ship. Come find me when you guys get back."

Sterling clipped the walkie back to his belt before making his way towards the stern.

"Almost done here. About to make our way back. See you in a few, Captain." Gage tossed his walkie down onto the sand and went back to helping Andrew set up the chuck box. Andrew was the crew cook and knew equipment better than anyone else. After a few more minutes, they had finished.

"Alright, guys. Your mobile kitchen is now ready for use," Gage called out to the group now gathered around a fire that Tim had prepared in the center of the site. "We've got these coolers filled with various foods. The blue one has fruits and veggies, the red one has a couple of lobsters and crab legs, and the bigger blue cooler has milk -- cream if you want some with your coffee -- and various other perishables."

"Wait! Weren't there more coolers?" Tim asked him before smiling and gently
nudging Henry teasingly.

"Spices are in the chuck box," Gage continued, trying not to laugh. "As well as
utensils, plates, and cooking equipment."

Gage spent the next few minutes going over instructions for the gear they had supplied for the group. Tim, Laura, Amber, and Henry politely paid attention. Nate was still passed out in his hammock.

Elizabeth was still back out on the beach with her camera enjoying the peace of being on her own. She didn't mind anyone in the group she found herself spending the weekend with, but she preferred to spend time on her own at the end of the day. She found the soft, dark colors of the horizon soothing, and she loved capturing them in photos.

She had been taking pictures throughout the day of all sorts of seagulls and dolphins, even the simplicity of the palm trees towering in the clear sky above. They were all beautiful to her.

Now, scanning the horizon, she found that their yacht too had an eerie beauty off in the distance. With the sun almost gone, the ship was not much more than a black silhouette in front of a dark orange backdrop that was all that remained of the day's light. The sun had disappeared under the horizon and she snapped a couple of pictures, zoomed in, and snapped a couple more.

She noticed something moving on the ship and she zoomed in further to see Captain Sterling at the back of the ship, doing what she assumed was maintenance on the ship to get ready for the night.

She found the scene oddly moving and snapped a few more pictures. She knew the captain was a veteran man of the sea who had spent years in the navy before retiring to the job he had now. Viewing him through her lens as a blacked-out figure at the tailing end of sunset while he "packed up" his ship, she couldn't help but see the shot she took as a metaphor for the captain in his retirement. It reminded her of her own grandfather in his
waning years, and she couldn't help but feel a tear in her eye.

Caught up in her emotion, she sat there just staring through the camera at the captain on the rear deck of the yacht and watching him as he knelt on the lowest portion of the rear deck and reached down into the water. He adjusted a couple of ropes that were hanging off the back end just above the water.

Elizabeth continued to watch the captain as a large dark shape came out of the water and latched onto him. Suddenly his arms and head disappeared into what she could only see as a large gullet before the shape receded back into the dark water, dragging the captain with it. Elizabeth stood up in shock, still staring at the ship, and screamed.

Chapter Four

Her blood curdling anguish rang through the air.

Laura jumped up from the sand where she was sitting and looked around to find its source. She spotted Elizabeth and ran over to her, the others now close behind.

"What happened? Are you alright?" Laura asked.

Elizabeth looked as pale as a ghost, her eyes wide and filled with tears. She had her hands cupped over her mouth and she was breathing heavily. Her camera lay in the sand beside her.

Laura knew she would never treat her equipment that recklessly. Something serious had happened.

"T-t-the captain…" she sobbed and fell to her knees. The rest of the crew, except for Nate, gathered around. Gage approached with Eric and Andrew behind him. All three had switched into "serious" mode, and Eric was carrying a first-aid kit, ready to tend to any emergency.

Gage knelt next to Elizabeth and looked her up and down, scanning for surface injuries.

"Hmm…" he said to the others. "She doesn't look hurt. What's wrong, ma'am? Can you tell us what happened?"

Elizabeth took deep breaths as she wiped her eyes. After a few seconds, she spoke.

"I-I was just…taking pictures and…the ship was out there and…I saw Captain Sterling and…something…I saw something…he got pulled in…" She started, but was unable to finish her sentence. She took more deep breaths and then continued. "I think
something got him. Something came out of the water and got him."
Gage looked quizzically at her and then stared out at the ship that sat quietly on the dark sea.

"What do you mean something got him?" he asked.

Elizabeth broke down into a sob briefly before reaching for her camera and fumbling with it, her hands trembling as she pressed a few buttons. She turned the screen towards Gage and showing him the photo of the ship out in the distance.

"I was taking pictures and I saw the captain on the rear deck of the ship. He was doing something in the back when something big grabbed him and pulled him in." She began pressing the little arrow button on the camera and the pictures changed, each shot zooming in closer to the ship. Captain Sterling appeared on the display, standing on the lower rear deck. The next shot showed him kneeling and reaching into the water.

She pressed the button again, but the screen went black. END OF LIBRARY showed in bold white letters in the center of the little screen.

"Are you sure? I mean it's been a long day for us all," Gage said.

"Are you sure he didn't just fall in?" Tim suggested. "Or maybe you took a page out of Nate's book and had one too many at the open bar," he added, trying to ease the tension.

"No!" Elizabeth spat at him, "I'm not drunk! I had one mimosa this morning. That's it."

Tim put his palms up to indicate he was backing off. He turned to face the ship in
the distance and stared in wonder, his hands on his hips.

Gage stood up and pulled a pair of small binoculars out of his cargo shorts pocket. He looked out at the rear of the yacht where Elizabeth had last seen the captain. He wasn't anywhere to be seen.

What could have grabbed him from out of the water, Gage puzzled. Maybe he really did just fall in by accident. It's entirely possible that he only fell in and then climbed back out of the water while everyone was focusing on Elizabeth. Still, something didn't feel right.

"Well, if something did happen," he began, "it's best we send someone over to check on the captain and make sure he's alright. Hopefully, he did just fall in. And hopefully climbed right back out. It's not like accidents don't happen."

He looked at Andrew and put his binoculars away.

"Andy, take the empty dinghy back over and check on the old man, would you? Take your radio and keep us posted."

Andrew nodded and headed back to where the dinghies were tied up and started getting one ready. Gage looked back at everyone else.

"Now, while he's doing that, I want everyone to remain calm and level-headed. We don't know for sure what happened, so there's no need for speculation until we get to the bottom of things. It's been a long day for us all, as I said, so it may be best if everyone
returned to their tents and got some rest."

The others seemed uneasy, but they reluctantly made their way back to the campsite. Elizabeth slowly gathered herself together, hung her camera back over her neck and got up.

She did her best to wipe away her tears.

Laura put her arm around her shoulders to comfort her as they walked back to the
tents together and reassured her that everything was going to be okay.

Tim went over and sat down next to the fire, followed by Henry who sat next to him. Amber sat across from them while Laura brought Elizabeth into her own tent to help calm her down.

Gage and Eric stayed back at the edge of the beach and talked to each other about what their next steps should be.

The camp was silent.

Tim stared into the fire. Henry spoke in almost a chanting speech and tried to reassure the others that everything was going to be okay. Tim thought it sounded like he was trying to reassure himself more than anything else.

"I think things are going to work out. I bet the captain is fine," Henry rattled on. "I bet he just fell in, like you said. As soon as Andy gets over to the ship, I think we'll find out everything is fine. We'll have a big laugh about it later. It's just one of those moments, you know?"

Amber felt Henry's anxiety, got up and sat down next to him, putting her head on his shoulder and wrapping her arm around him.

"I bet you're right. Everything's going to be okay," she reaffirmed.

His face turned red as he stopped talking. He felt too flustered to say anything else.

Instead, he let himself enjoy her comfort.

After a while Tim finally broke the silence.

"Maybe. I don't know. I don't want to get too comfortable until we find out what happened. If we lost Captain Sterling, we might have to end up fending for ourselves on this
island for a little longer than we thought." He tossed another thick branch into the fire.

Amber shot a look at him. "What do you mean?"

"I mean," he replied, "that if the captain is no longer with us, who is going to get us back home? The yacht's crew seem competent, but do they know how to sail a whole yacht on their own?"

The redness in Henry's face had vanished and his cheeks returned to their former pale complexion. He hadn't thought of what Tim had said, and the idea of being stranded on an island in the middle of nowhere made him feel sick.

Amber thought for a second and then said, "I don't know. I bet they know how. If it comes down to it and they really need a fourth person to help get us home, I mean, there are six of us. I bet if we all worked together we'd be able to get us back to the mainland." She paused, thinking again for a second. "Plus, even if they aren't able to drive the yacht, we could always just get ourselves back to it and call for some help or for something, like a helicopter, to pick us up!" She felt the tension in Henry's shoulders ease as she said that. She had even made herself feel a little better. There's always a way out, she thought.

"Ah, but it's not that simple though, is it?" Tim said. He pulled out a cell phone from his pocket and waggled it. "We have absolutely no cell service out here. Total dead zone."

Amber frowned, got up, and made her way back into her tent. After some rummaging sounds, she came back out with her phone in hand. She stood in front of the
others and pressed the button to turn it on. After a minute, her expression saddened me.

"I've got nothing out here either, not even a single bar. I was planning on posting my vacation pics on my Pixogram account."

She tossed her phone back back over into her tent and plopped back down next to Henry.

Tim hid his smile. Amber was a grown adult, maybe a little younger than most of the group there, but the way she conducted herself was childish sometimes. Right now, all he could see was that she was a pouting teenager who just had her phone taken away from her.

"At any rate," Tim continued, "there's no point in thinking too far ahead. We just have to deal with things as they come."

Silence once again filled the beach.

Gage and Eric who had moved further along and down the beach to where Andrew was getting his dinghy ready for departure.

"So, assuming everything is fine, once we hear back from Andy, we'll take the second dinghy back ourselves," Eric said to Gage. "We're done here for the night anyways."

Gage confirmed his plan.

Andrew, now with the boat untied and the rope in his hands, asked Gage "…and if everything isn't fine?"

Gage didn't have an answer, not right away at least. Truthfully, he hadn't really thought that far ahead, and he wasn't sure he was even ready to think about taking command of everyone if something really had happened to Sterling.

"If everything isn't fine…" he started, carefully thinking about what to say, "…then our priority is making sure our guests are safe and back on board the ship. I think that's what the captain would want."

Andrew nodded and slipped on a life vest, clipped his radio to it and began pushing the dinghy out into the water. As the tide took the boat, he hopped in and started fumbling with the propeller engine. It whirred to life, and he set off back toward the ship.

Gage watched as he sailed off into the dark abyss of the night, the hum of the motor slowly fading out into the distance until only the sound of the tide hitting the beach filled the air.

Eric walked back to the campsite to inform the group what to expect, as well as to reassure them that things were going to be okay. Gage stayed and stood firmly at the edge of the beach, waiting for the radio call from Andrew that would shed some light on their situation.

Minutes passed and Gage felt an uneasy feeling grow in his chest. The ship was anchored only a little distance out from the shore, and it really shouldn't take more than a few minutes for Andrew to get there, especially since they'd emptied the dinghy.

More minutes passed. Gage knew Andrew should have at least made it to the ship by now. Maybe he was just having a laugh with the captain, Gage thought, and everything was fine. He probably forgot about the apparent urgency of the situation back on the island once he found Sterling and hadn't called Gage yet.

Those few minutes turned into ten more. Those ten turned into a half hour. A half hour eventually became a full hour.

Gage couldn't stand it anymore. Something wasn't right. He pulled out his walkie and radioed to Andrew. Maybe by now the captain would answer instead.

"Hello… anyone? This is Gage calling anyone on the ship. Andy, are you there?" There was no reply.

"Gage to Andy, do you read me? Were you able to find Captain Sterling?" Again, nothing but static on the radio.

Eric had walked back to Gage, his walkie in his hand. He knew something was up, and he too was starting to get worried.

"Maybe it's your radio," he said to Gage with a slight hint of false hope in his voice.

"Lemme try."

He brought his walkie up to his mouth and spoke.

"This is the second mate, Eric, here. Does anyone hear me? A reply from anyone would be really nice right about now…"

Gage stared out toward the yacht, but the darkness now enveloped everything within a few feet of the shore. There was no moon and Gage realized the storm clouds were probably now covering the sky. The night was too dark to see the yacht, they weren't getting word about their captain and they had now lost contact with the third mate.

It was time to figure out something else to do.

Gage made one more desperate attempt to reach anyone on the walkie-talkie who might have been listening on the other side of the black veil that obscured their sight of their ship.

“Andrew, please respond. It’s been about…” he looked at his watch. “It’s been over an hour now, please get back to us to let us know you and Captain Sterling are okay...”

Sterling is okay…

Gage looked at Eric, surprised.

“Did you say something?” Eric shook his head.

“No. I think that was just you on my radio. Let me turn it off, quick.” Eric twisted the knob on his radio until the little static that remained had died out. Gage continued speaking message.

“Andrew, if we don’t hear back from you in the next couple of minutes, we’re going to have to cut this trip short and get everyone back on the ship. Please respond…”

“Ship. Please respond…”

Gage looked back at Eric, who also now had a puzzled look on his face.

“It’s not me this time. I shut my radio off.”

Gage stared at him and brought his walkie up to his mouth again.

“Hello?” he spoke clearly.

”…Hello?” came the echo.

It did not come from Eric’s walkie after all. It sounded like it was coming from… Gage turned and stared back out into the dark waves.

“Andy?” he called again, closely followed by another unexpected echo.

”Andy?”

It was definitely coming from out over the water, but it was too dark to see from where. Eric read Gage’s mind and ran back to the campsite to rummage through the supplies before returning with a large flashlight.

He flicked it on and pointed it out into the dark and scanned back and forth over
the rippling surface of the ocean.

"Say something again." Eric said, looking around.

Gage reluctantly brought his radio up to his lips again, frightened of what they might discover.

"This is Gage…hello?"

"This is Gage…hello?" came the response.

Eric pointed his light in the direction the echo had come from. They still couldn't see anything. He slowly moved the beam across different sections of water, searching
for…anything.

Suddenly Gage spotted something.

"Wait!" he exclaimed, pointing at one wave out in the water twenty feet in front of him. "What's that?"

Eric moved the light to where he was pointing and the two of them saw something standing out as clear as day in the dark waves…an orange object, gently floating amongst the waves.

"What is that?" Gage repeated.

He looked behind on the beach and spotted a long piece of driftwood. He picked it up and held it out over the water, attempting to pull the strange orange mass closer to shore.

As the object got closer, they both recognized it.

It was Andy's life-vest, and clipped to the front of it was a black, shiny radio.

Eric audibly breathed a sigh of relief.

"Man, Andy can be such a klutz sometimes. Looks like he dropped his vest on his way over. It would explain why at least he isn't getting back to us. He's probably still looking for another radio on the ship."

Gage's eyes widened and Eric heard him gulp.

"I…don't think he made it back to the ship…" Gage sputtered.

"What? Why not? I mean, why else would he have taken off his vest if he didn't make it back?"

The branch of driftwood now trembled slightly in Gage's hands. He pulled the vest ashore and let the waves recede from it, revealing the entire vest to Eric.

"He didn't make it back," Gage said.

Eric finally saw what he meant. It was true. Andrew had never taken the vest off in the first place. The vest was still puffed out with his torso, but all that could be seen in the armholes were dark pink and red, chunky surfaces. All that remained of Andrew was now there lying on the sand in front of them, wrapped in orange nylon.

Chapter Five

Gage stood still on the sand, too stunned to speak. The beam of Eric's flashlight that had rested on Andrew's torso began to shake. Gage looked at Eric and saw that even in the dark of night, his face looked sickly pale.

"Oh, man…" Eric exhaled. He took a couple steps back and collapsed to his knees, dropping the flashlight. He vomited into the sand. Gage tossed the branch aside and backed up, put his hands to his face and took a couple of deep breaths. Within the span of a few hours, they had evidently lost the captain and the third mate of the crew. That meant the first mate, Gage, was now in charge. He
knew he couldn't afford to lose it right now. Everything rested on his shoulders.
"Okay…okay. First things first…" Gage began to pull himself together. "I think we
should bury Andrew. Or, at least, what's left of him…"
Eric nodded slowly. "Okay…" he finally said and got back up on his feet. "What do
we tell everyone?" he asked.
Gage hadn't thought that far ahead yet, but already he found himself facing the hard questions. He knew he had to hit the ground running in his new position of leadership.

"I think… we don't have to say anything. Not yet. We don't want them to panic. Let's just let them sleep through the night and we'll tell them tomorrow, after we get everyone back to the boat. For now…"

Gage looked over at the campsite, the faint glow of the fire illuminating the small number of bodies huddled around it. Only two figures remained there. The rest must have

gone to bed, or at least tried to. That was good, Gage decided.
He looked over at Eric. He could tell he wasn't doing well, but was trying his best to put on a brave face. He felt bad for him. Eric was always quick to crack a joke to ease others' tension, but neither of them had been through anything like this, and Gage could see it was definitely getting to him.

"Let's head back over to camp. You stay with them. I'll grab a compact shovel and take care of the – of Andrew…" he said, almost forgetting that the hunk of amorphous mass in front of them was, only a few hours ago, their coworker.

Eric nodded. He looked down at the torso in the sand and caught himself as his gag reflex kicked in again.

Together, the two of them walked back to the campsite in silence.

The fire had shrunk from its former size and was now only warming the last two remaining around it, Amber and Henry. Eric sat himself down across from the two of them and reached for another chunk of wood that sat in a pile behind him and tossed it into the flames. He sat there, still, and continued to stare into the orange flickering of the fire.

Henry woke, and seeing the absent look in Eric's eyes, a concerned look came over his face.

"What happened?" he asked. "Did you hear back from Captain Sterling?"

Eric looked at Henry, then at Gage, who looked back at him briefly before taking
control of the conversation.

"We are still waiting to hear back from Andy, but things are looking up. The fact that he hasn't contacted us yet tells me that he likely found Captain Sterling and is probably attending to his wounds, assuming he got hurt on his fall off the ship. That's policy on our ship if someone gets hurt. Gotta' take care of the wounded first."

He couldn't tell these Hollywood people the truth. Not yet. They had already spent all day out on the ocean and it would be best if they were able to clear their heads and get some rest for the night. He'll tell them tomorrow, when everyone had time to process the two deaths clearly.

Gage stood and walked over to the chuck box and opened it up, pretending to inspect everything as he quietly slid the compact shovel out from one of its compartments. After a few more minutes of browsing, he shut the box and headed back to the beach to begin his daunting task.

* * *

The next morning the beach was quiet except for the seagulls that flew back and forth over the calm lapping of the waves on the beach.

Amber was the first to rise from her slumber, or so she initially thought. She sat up in her tent and stretched. "What am I going to have for breakfast?" she thought. "I could kill for some avocado toast right now. Maybe a French vanilla coffee, some strawberries…"

Her thought process stopped when everything started coming back to her. Somehow, after a good sleep, she had forgotten about their unusual situation overnight. She looked around her tent, digging through her blankets and pillows until she found her phone and turned it on. It was almost dead, and she still didn't have any service. She tossed it back down onto her pillow in frustration.

She climbed out of her tent and was greeted by the bright morning sun surrounded
by a vast, clear blue sky. It brightened her mood immediately.

She gazed around the campsite. Everyone's tent was closed up, although there were still red coals lying in the fire pit. Somebody either had stayed up late tending to the fire, or someone had gotten up early and tended to it, at least temporarily.

She looked around again. The two yacht crewmates were both slumped over
underneath a nearby tree, still asleep.

They look so cute, she thought.

Then she spotted, just to the left of the tree, a single lawn chair sitting on the beach in the sun. A dirty blond head poked up from it. She walked over and found Nate lounging in the sun. He had a cup of coffee in one hand and a joint in the other. He was wearing his shades, so she couldn't tell if he was actually awake.

"Good morning, beautiful, he said.

Guess he's awake, Amber realized.

"Hey," she replied. She wasn't expecting his compliment, but she did always love
getting one.

"There's some coffee in the coffee press if you want some. If not, there's still some hot water in the kettle, and I think we have some tea in the box."

He took a long puff from his joint and held it in before slowly exhaling the smoke. He coughed twice and rubbed his eyes behind his dark glasses.. He looked at Amber, staring at him with mixed emotions, and he held up his hand as if to offer her a hit.

Without hesitation she took the joint and inhaled deeply. She was no stranger to partying. She exhaled her first hit through her nose with smoke coming out of both nostrils before she went in for another hit, this time an even longer drag than the first.

"Hey, now, don't Bogart that stick on me," Nate said, sporting a subtle grin. He was impressed.

Amber handed the joint back to him and calmly exhaled again, without even needing to clear her throat.

"Where did you get this? Did you bring it? It's good stuff," she said.

Nate put the joint in his mouth before digging out a red and white cardboard pack of Marlboros from his Bahama shirt pocket. He flipped it open and showed Amber another half a dozen rolled up joints. He flipped it closed, stuffed it back into his pocket, pulled the joint from his lips, and took a sip from his coffee.

"You seem pretty relaxed this morning," Amber said.

"That's why we're here, toots," he responded, relaxing his head on the chair once
again. "For at least today and most of tomorrow, I'm not doing jack."

"But what about the captain?"

"What about him?"

She remembered that Nate had passed out in his hammock well before the shocking events the night before. How was she supposed to tell him? What was she supposed to tell him? She didn't even really know what happened yet.

"Nate, last night… Liz saw…we think something happened to Captain Sterling."

Nate turned his head towards her and pulled his shades down and stared at her
quizzically.

"Liz said she saw something come out of the water and grab him from the yacht. She saw it through her camera." Even as she said it, it almost sounded silly to her. What would come out of the water to grab someone on a yacht in the middle of nowhere?

Nate sat up and stared at her before looking out at the yacht sitting peacefully on the horizon.

"What? Something came out of the water and grabbed him from the yacht?" Amber nodded.

He looked at her again, analyzing. After a long minute, he finally spoke.

"So…let's say that something actually happened to the captain…what are we going to do about it? Gage and his second hand don't seem too concerned about it the way they're cuddled up next to each other over there."

Amber looked at Gage and Eric, still passed out in slumber. In a weird way Nate had a point. Sort of.

"Well, they sent the chef guy out on one of the boats last night to go investigate, but I don't see him around anywhere."

She looked around the small island as if to look for him, but to no avail. Nate looked back out at the yacht.

"And we never heard back from him?" he asked.

"I don't know. I think we all went to bed before they found anything."

Nate thought for a moment. Couldn't he have just one day of rest and relaxation, he thought. There's always something. He took another sip from his coffee and stuck the joint back in his mouth.

"Well, until we hear something new, I'm just going to sit back and kick it. This is my vacation, and I will enjoy as much of it as I can."

He lay back down in his chair and took another long drag from the joint.

Amber looked at him admiringly. Here we are, she thought, nearly stranded on an island in the middle of nowhere with our captain and one crewmate not accounted for since yesterday and he is as relaxed as could be.

She turned and started to walk back to the campsite, but stopped herself and looked back at Nate.

"What kind of coffee?" she asked him.

"Hazelnut. There's cream and other fixin's in the big blue cooler," he called back,

lazily pointing his hand backwards in the general direction of the camp site.

Amber smiled and headed towards the kitchen box.

For most of the morning Henry had kept himself tucked away in the safety of his tent, all bundled up in his sleeping bag. He hadn't been doing well. He really hadn't liked the way Eric and Gage had subtly conversed through their body language last night. That one look on Eric's face, though brief, had struck Henry in his core. What was in that face? Shock? Trauma? Fear? All of the above?

Whatever it was, he recognized it, as he himself was no stranger to those ill feelings. Life has not been easy to him, and it wasn't until he was able to get his job as an assistant director that things had finally started going his way. Or at least, they had started to. Once again, he now thought, life had a funny way of messing with him.

After finally getting himself out of his own head, he sat up and put his face in his hands, massaging and stretching every inch of it. He took a deep breath and climbed out of his sleeping bag, threw some clothes on, and emerged from the safe space of his tent.

He wasn't sure what he expected to see, but it sure wasn't what he saw…normalcy, to an extent. Laura and Amber sat quietly by the campfire. Two frying pans lay on top of the hot coals. One held half a dozen eggs, the other had several strips of bacon. Both sizzled and sputtered grease out of the pans and into the fire.

Amber looked up from her cup of coffee and smiled at Henry.

"Good morning, Henry," she said softly. Her sunglasses were perched on top of her head and he got his first clear look at her beautiful, dark brown eyes. His heart leaped in his chest, but before he had a chance to say something he knew would be embarrassing, Laura spoke up.

"Good morning, Henry. I got some breakfast going if you like eggs and bacon. Did you sleep well?" She pointed over at the kitchen box. "And there's some fresh coffee if you haven't fully woken up yet."

He liked Laura. She was one of the few people on the set of Crabzilla who had been decent to him. He smiled back and nodded before heading over to the kitchen box to pour himself a cup of coffee. As he mixed in his cream and sugar, he continued his scan of the scene.

Nate was lounging in the sun on a beach chair, a coffee cup pressed into the sand and an arm hung over one of the arm rests. It looked like he could have been asleep already. Was he going to sleep this entire trip, Henry wondered. At this rate, Nate wasn't even going to find out about the situation of the captain missing until they were already back at Benoa Port.

Elizabeth sat on the beach further down the bank. It looked like she was cleaning her camera, probably attempting to get sand particles out of the lens and nooks. She seemed to have pulled herself together at least a little bit since last night, and she seemed thoroughly invested in the cleaning of her equipment.

Over by the tree that anchored the remaining dinghy were Eric and Gage. They were having a heated discussion while Gage rummaged through the compartments of the boat. Henry didn't like the looks of it, and he thought it best to stay out of it for now. They were technically in charge now, so he had to trust that they were going to figure out what the next step for them all would be.

"Well if it isn't sleepy head Henry!" a gruff voice called out. Henry turned around to see Tim walking towards him, a fishing pole in one hand and a tackle box in the other. Henry gave him a look.

"Sleepy head Henry?" he questioned.

Tim shrugged. "That was the best I could come up with. It was either that or hit-the hay-Henry, but that didn't feel as smooth. But you're up now! Care to join me for some mid-morning fishing?"

Tim was beaming in a way that Henry hadn't seen before. It was unusual to see him in such a good mood, especially given the circumstances. Tim was an excellent director, but it just now became clear to Henry that Tim was truly in his element when surrounded by the natural world.

Realizing this made Henry feel better, as not only did they still have the ship crew,
but they also had survivalist Tim.

"Yeah, that sounds pretty good right about now," Henry said. *Some peaceful fishing would help him take his mind off the serious matters at hand,* he thought.

Together, they walked off towards the beach only a few meters down the bank from where Nate slumbered in his chair.

"What are we trying to catch?" Henry asked.

"Lunch!" Tim replied without any hesitation. "And maybe if we're lucky…dinner!" Henry could tell how passionate Tim was about fishing. He guessed that Tim was the kind of guy who knew how to gut, scale, and clean a fish and have it ready to eat in a matter of minutes, and with a minimum amount of cooking supplies on hand, too.

Tim found a spot in the wet sand and set down his tackle box. He took a moment to gaze at his vast, blue hunting ground and he then tilted his head back and looked straight up to the sky.

"I thank you in advance, almighty mother nature, and I am ever so grateful for all you provide. I ask in return to give me a nice, big ole' tuna. Or even a squid. I could go for some calamari tonight." .

Woah, Henry thought. *He really was serious about this.* Was he praying?

Henry continued to be baffled by the relaxed and care-free boss whom he had only
ever gotten to know in the studio.

After speaking his word to mother nature, Tim crouched down and opened up his tackle, fitting his line with what appeared to be… crab meat? He looked up at Henry and
grinned a big, toothy grin.

"Scraps from the seafood buffet. This kind of stuff makes for excellent bait, especially out here on the big blue." He stood up and waded out into the water, ready to cast his line. "That's how it is out there in the real world, too, kid," he continued. "Catch one fish, use that to catch a bigger fish that will land you an even bigger one. It's a dog-eat-dog world. Or, I guess in this case, a fish-eat-fish world…"

He continued on with a speech about the ways of the world and life and all of its
glories and flaws, all the while casting and reeling, casting and reeling.

Henry couldn't help but chuckle. He could probably walk away right now and return a half hour later and still hear him talking. He didn't mind, though. It was nice to hear him speak so passionately about something. Henry sat down in the sand and listened.

Chapter Six

"I mean, what are we supposed to do? This isn't something we can just 'wait out.' We haven't heard from the captain or Andrew since last night. You and I should have
already been back on the ship by this morning."

Eric continued to bombard Gage with his unrelenting questions while he inspected
the rope that kept the dinghy tied down. He had to do something to stay busy.

"I don't know, Eric. We haven't exactly been in this kind of situation before," Gage responded calmly and then paused. He was trying hard to keep a clear head, but Eric's frantic monologue wasn't helping.

"If you ask me," Eric continued, "we should just take this thing with everyone in it to the ship and get ourselves back to Benoa. We could probably pilot it ourselves, and we
could have them help us if we needed to."

Gage shook his head no.

"The two of us? We could pilot the ship alone, and the others wouldn't be of any help to us. They wouldn't know what they were doing, and it would take too long to teach
them to do anything."

Eric silently agreed, although he didn't like to. He knew what Gage was talking about, too, and he also had noticed the grayish clouds earlier looming off in the distance. He looked up at the horizon. They were distant enough that none of the film crew seemed to pay any attention to them. Either that or they just didn't understand the serious undertone of what those clouds meant.

"You think it's coming our way?" Eric finally asked as he pointed to the dark clouds along the far horizon.

"I think… it could. It wasn't supposed to. The captain and I heard a broadcast over the radio about it, saying it was heading southbound. Sterling wasn't worried about it. He just brushed it off. He said if we were going to see it at all, it would be on our way back to port."

Gage paused. He couldn't keep doing this mindless busy work. He looked out at the clouds lingering menacingly on the horizon sky.

"But I saw them earlier this morning," Gage said, "and they haven't shifted much in either direction. They've only grown slightly. That tells me they actually are coming our way."

Eric nodded.

"Just what we needed," he muttered weakly. Things were not going their way. *Worst gig they had ever taken*, he thought. He needed to think what to do next. It was up to him and Gage to get these people back to the boat. Back to safety. Hell, one now guilty part of him wanted to save himself most.

That's a normal response, he thought to himself. *That's just my natural survival instincts kicking in. I can still help these people.*

He gazed around the small patch of land they found themselves on, trying to mentally take inventory of everything they had at their disposal. He looked at the campsite and for a minute watched a few of the celebrities enjoy their morning breakfast, oblivious to what might be in store for them.

Suddenly he heard a commotion out on the beach. He could see the director, Timothy, waist deep in the water holding a curved fishing rod. He was excitedly wrestling what must have been a big catch. The little guy whose name he couldn't remember sat in the sand watching.

Nate, who had woken from his dazed slumber, was making his way over to stand next to the assistant director. They both began rooting for Tim. The three of them seemed
to have forgotten all about the dire situation and were really enjoying themselves.

Eric smiled as a bittersweet feeling washed over him. He wished he could be in the dark like they were. He wished he could forget about the bloody, disfigured mass of a corpse that had once been his coworker and friend. He felt sick just picturing it again.

Before getting too lost in his traumatic recollection, a loud splashing sound brought him back to reality. He saw that Timothy was no longer standing in the water. In a matter of seconds he had simply vanished.

Nate and the little guy had gone silent on the beach. Nate pulled his sunglasses off
his face looked confused.

Was he imagining things, Nate wondered to himself? Was Tim actually there fishing just a moment before, or had he just smoked and drank more than he should have this morning?

"...Tim?" Henry called out hesitantly.

Nate looked down, as if he had somehow already forgotten that he was sitting there. Maybe he did go a bit overboard with the substances he'd been consuming. Although, the fact that Henry was still sitting there meant that he probably was indeed just watching Tim fish.

Now Nate was really confused.

Henry got up off the sand, worried. Tim still hadn't re-surfaced yet. Was he messing

around? Did he lose his footing? No, he had submerged too quickly for that.

All at once Tim finally bobbed up to the surface in a frenzy, thrashing around in the
water as if he were in the middle of an intense wrestling match.

"You slimy son-of-a..." he yelled.

Suddenly he was pulled back under.

Henry started moving towards him and Gage and Eric ran over to Henry and Nate from the other side of the beach. Amber and Laura had started walking over from the
campsite.

Amber now had her hands covering her mouth.

"We have to do something!" Henry yelled in increasing panic. He looked around him and found a large stick lying on the beach. He grabbed it and ran over to the violent
commotion in the water and waded in.

"Tim! Tim, grab hold!" he shouted over the splashing and held out the stick.

Gage came up behind him.

"Get back!" Gage yelled and yanked Henry back from the water.

Henry landed on his butt in the wet sand just as a gray mass emerged from the water snapping noisily at his feet. All Henry could see was a large, gaping hole lined with endless rows of sharp white teeth. Henry froze.

The large maw was mere inches away and was attempting to shimmy itself along the sand closer to him. Henry yelled and started kicking at the snout of the beast, trying his best to keep his feet out of the deadly entrance to its gullet.

He felt hands grab him from behind and lift him back from the water's edge.

Nate and Eric had both grabbed hold of him from under his shoulders and dragged him further up the sandy beach.

Henry could finally see what the toothy maw belonged to. Thrashing on the beach in front of him was eighteen feet of meaty shark. Its beady black eyes stared directly at him, almost taunting him to come closer so it could take a bite out of him.

A minute later, apparently realizing that its potential meal was going to stay out of reach, the shark wiggled its way back into the tide and disappeared into the water as quickly as it had appeared.

Everything went silent.

No one was yelling. There were no more sounds of splashing in the ocean.

Soon the seagulls started squawking again and the waves gently crashed onto the beach as if nothing had happened.

Henry tried getting up, but his legs were trembling too much. Gage kneeled down
next to him.

"It's okay, man. You're okay. It didn't get you. Just… take a second and breathe.
You're alive. You're going to be okay."

"But… but… that thing… it was… how…?" Henry said through his deep breaths, unable to form a proper sentence. Suddenly his eyes widened. "Where's Tim?"

Everyone brought their gaze back to the calm water. Where Tim had stood and
fought for his life, nothing was left but a red mist on the surface of the water.

"Woah," Nate said. "He's just… gone."

Seeing the attack had spared him up. He knew something had happened the night before, but he barely knew the details and he hadn't really been interested. He had virtually passed out by the time they had first arrived on the island.

Now, seeing this first hand, losing not only the director he had been working with for months, but narrowly losing the assistant director at the same time, Nate became focused suddenly. Realizing he had just helped pull Henry back from meeting the same fate as Tim, he just shook his head once, turned around, and made his way towards camp. Laura saw the empty look on his face and touched his arm as he walked by, but her hand elicited no response.

"Nate…" she said softly. He didn't look back.

"It's alright. Just…" Gage started. "…he just needs time to process. I think we all do…" he trailed off.

Eric frowned at Gage. "What we need," he began in a rising tone, "is to get off this god-forsaken island! That's the third person we've lost here, and it hasn't even been a full day yet! What's going to happen to the rest of us when that storm gets here?"

He was yelling by the end of his exclamation, but he didn't care. He couldn't stand sitting around anymore.

"Third?" Laura asked. Amber looked at her.

"I'm going to get the boat ready for departure," Eric said and marched off towards the anchored dinghy. "Whoever's not on it in ten minutes is staying on the island. Leave everything behind but the clothes on your back. We are getting out of here."

Gage grabbed his arm and held him back. "Stop!" he said firmly.

Eric turned around with anger in his eyes.

"Take your hand off me, Gage," he warned.

"What do you mean 'third person' we've lost?" Amber demanded.

"Not now," Gage responded bluntly.

Eric pulled Gage's arm away.

"You know what happened?" he yelled at Amber. "Andrew's dead too. We found him washed up on shore last night. Or what was left of him anyways. Nothing more than his chest." He turned directly to Gage. "We buried him, too. He buried our friend last night. All that food you guys were indulging yourselves in yesterday? Andrew made it. And now what's left of him is the size of a pillow and buried under a pile of sand…"

Eric collapsed to his knees, placed his hands on his face, and broke down in tears.

His cries filled the quiet void around him.

After several minutes Laura knelt down next to him and embraced him, not saying a word.

Amber broke the silence. "So…what do we do now? Do we just leave and get back on the boat? I feel like that's what we should do…"

But she looked at Gage expectantly.

He shook his head. "We can't. It's not safe right now." He lifted his hand and
pointed out at the sea before them. "We're dealing with a shiver now."

Everyone looked where he pointed. It took them all a moment, but one by one they began to notice half a dozen fins protruding from the water and circling around in almost
perfectly synced routines, like prison guards keeping an eye on their captives.

"A shiver…? Sharks?" Laura asked, looking out at them.

"Yes, a group of sharks, though it's impossible to tell just how many are out there. It doesn't matter though. If we take that boat out there with that waiting for us," he said, pointing at the sharks, "then they're just going to swarm us and destroy the dinghy. We still haven't seen the boat

Andy took out last night, so I have to assume they sunk it and got to him while he was swimming his way over to the yacht."

Eric continued sobbing. Every emotion he'd been holding back for the last twelve hours had finally caught up with him in an epic release. He was mad at Gage for not taking any action. He was terrified that they only had one boat left to get them all to safety. He was angry with himself for wanting to save himself. Most of all he was too upset from having seen Andrew's remains. He had been someone he had worked closely with for the last two years.

Laura stood up and stuck her face in Gage's. She was not afraid to let her emotions
show, and right now, her emotion was anger.

"So, you're telling me not one, but two of your men died last night, assuming Captain Sterling met the same fate as the chef…and you didn't tell any of us then? What gives you the right to keep us in the dark on something like this?"

She started shoving Gage backwards, but he didn't react. That made her even
angrier.

"If you had told us, we could have done something last night. We could have called for help!" She pointed towards the spot in the water where Tim had stood moments before.

"We could have kept everyone safe and out of the water!"

She finished and tears began to form in her eyes. She spun around began to pace back and forth along the beach, trying to calm herself down, when she spotted Elizabeth
further down along the sand, curled up as if she were trying to hide herself from the world.

Laura stopped pacing. Elizabeth had taken all night recuperating from what she had witnessed the night before only to have a front row

seat to another attack today. This time she had the personal loss of someone she had known and worked with.
Laura sighed and turned back to Gage.

"Look. You figure out a way to get us back home, and you do it fast."

She walked over to comfort Elizabeth, once again.

Amber sat down in the sand next to Henry, still in shock from the rapid events that had unfolded moments before, and hugged him. Normally Henry would have turned a
bright shade of red within seconds, but he had checked out from the present reality.
Gage stood over Eric and held out his hand in an offer to help him to his feet. Eric
finally grabbed it and got up while wiping the tears from his eyes.

"Come on," Gage spoke. "Let's go figure out what we're going to do."

Down the beach Laura spoke softly to Elizabeth, her arm around her in a close
embrace.

"It's okay, honey. You're okay. Everything's going to be okay."

Elizabeth just shook her head back and forth. She stifled another sob and tried to
regain control of her breathing.

"No, it's not. We're going to… we're going to die here… just like Tim and… and…"

She lost control and started crying again. Laura pulled her in closer, doing her best to console her and let her cry into her shoulder.

Laura then glanced out at the water, watching the occasional shark fin quietly pass by, and noticed the storm. What had begun as a small patch of clouds early that morning far out on the horizon had grown to a gathering of dark gray masses in the sky, inching ever so slowly towards their island. Her brow furrowed.

"Hey, Amber?" she called out.

Amber looked up at her, and Laura silently pointed at Elizabeth and mouthed
"'Come here."

Amber understood this as her way to say, "Come take over for a sec," and she nodded. She squeezed Henry's hand before getting up and heading over to the two women.

After turning Elizabeth over to Amber, Laura stood and briskly followed the two shipmates to catch up with them.

"Hey!" she called out.

Gage and Eric turned around, clearly mid conversation. Laura approached and
pointed at the cluster of ominous clouds over the ocean.

"Is that going to hit us?"

Eric's eyes widened and darted over to Gage, who only took a moment to
contemplate his response.

"It's… likely." He looked out at the storm himself.

"Are we going to be okay?" she asked and followed up with, "I mean, we have tents. Or, at least, most of us do. But something tells me that's going to be a bit more than just rain."

Gage looked at Laura. He was surprised that she was such an observant one. He
decided not to beat around the bush with her. She was too smart.

"You're right. That is definitely going to be more than some light rain. What you are looking at out there is a cyclone, and if it maintains on a steady course our way, we're going to have to deal with more than just sharks."

"A cyclone?" she repeated.

Eric cleared his throat. "Yeah, it's like a hurricane but…"

Laura held up her hand at him. "I know what a cyclone is. What I don't know is how anyone cleared this trip while there was a freaking…" She closed her eyes and composed herself before getting too worked up. "…while there was a cyclone out here where we planned on camping."

"We've been loosely keeping an eye on it," Gage retorted. "Captain Sterling said it wasn't going to interfere with our trip. It was supposed to keep heading south and we wouldn't have even seen it, but things changed. No one can really predict when a storm changes direction."

"So? What are we supposed to do? Clearly we can't take the boats back to the yacht with those sharks out there. Do we just tie everything down and hope we don't get carried off in the waves?"

"No, no. The last report we heard about the storm said it was a category one with potential to become a category two. It would take a category five storm to have enough waves to lift us off the ground."

There was silence, and Laura stared at him, waiting for more.

"But?" Laura guessed.

"But," Gage continued hesitantly, "while we don't have to worry about getting lifted away, we will have to worry about going under." He gestured around the island as if to showcase it as a prize on a game show. "This place isn't even technically an island. It's hardly more than a sandbar that emerges every so often. If that storm gets too close to us, this whole little beach goes under."

"And if that happens," Eric added, "we're going to have a bit more company on our campgrounds." He nodded out to the water at the circling fins.

The trio stood in silence contemplating the idea of losing the only ground they could stand on to a bunch of hungry sharks.

Laura looked around, searching for something, anything that could help them survive. She looked at the campsite, empty save for Nate lying in his hammock. He looked more in shock than relaxed, she decided. For a moment, she felt bad for him. It was obvious that watching Tim get mauled had broken through the rough and tough façade he always displayed. She had almost forgotten that it was a front. He was, after all, an actor.

Her gaze traveled from his hammock to up the tree it was tied to until she reached
the palm fronds at the top.

"What about those trees?" she asked.

Eric looked at her quizzically. "What about them?"

Gage looked at the trees, back at Laura, and then back at the trees. Laura could see
the gears turning in his head. He was catching on.

"Clearly the trees have had enough of a foundation here to withstand all manner of rising tides in the past," she said. "So, what if we just climb them when the water level
rises?"

Gage nodded thoughtfully, sizing up the trees as if taking their measurements.

"It could work. Potentially…if everyone could endure sitting up there for an extended period of time."

"Well, we could cut some notches into the tree," Eric suggested. "Maybe a couple for us to hold onto the trees and a couple further down, slap some sticks into 'em, and have something to stand on?".

Gage liked the idea.

“And we have some emergency ropes,” he said. ”We could tie everyone to the trees in a sort of safety harness.”

Gage and Eric then started bouncing ideas off each other, quickly making plans on
how to ensure the safety of the group.

Afterward Gage walked over to the others, now gathered around the campsite, and assigned each of them a job to do. Time was of the essence, he stressed, and Eric and Laura were tasked with climbing each of the six trees on the island and carving slots into them.

“You know,” Eric called down to Gage as he chipped away at the side of the tree he hung on to. “One of us is going to have to share a tree. There’s seven of us.”

“I…” Gage started before he was interrupted.

“Henry and I can share a tree!” Amber called out. She and Henry were busy cleaning up the campsite, undoing tents and packing up the chuck box. “We’re both the lightest people here. We can share one!”

Henry, even though the matter was literally of life or death, blushed at the idea that he was going to be spending some intimate, although probably uncomfortable, time with
her.

Gage shrugged. “Okay.”

Nate and Elizabeth were busy preparing the rope. They took turns unraveling and
cutting ten foot sections of it and preparing each section at the base of each tree. Nate cut through the final bit of thick rope and wiped his brow, sweating profusely. He pulled his flask out of his pocket and held it in the air for a moment while he observed his fellow
cohorts in action.

He watched as his wife, who had grown distant from him in the last few years, scaled the tree effortlessly and cut holes into the bark.

Her sleeves were rolled up, displaying her firmly built muscles. He smiled and took a swig, remembering why he had found her so attractive all those years ago. She was not afraid to do the work that needed to be done.

"Alright," Gage called out, interrupting Nate's train of thought. "I think everyone should wear a life jacket when we're up in the trees. They'll add additional padding against the rope, and should any one of us fall, we can at least stay…"

He stopped when he felt a gentle tap on the top of his head. His heart sank as he instantly recognized what it was. He looked out at the horizon, now considerably darker. The storm couldn't have been more than a few miles out. The waves in the tide were no longer as calm as they had been. The dark clouds had finally reached the island, and when he looked up at them floating menacingly above, he felt a second tap, this time hitting his forehead.

Tap…tap… tap tap… taptaptaptap… The rain had arrived.

Gage shouted, "Let's get a move on, people. I'm going to go grab some branches for us to stand on and then I want to start getting us tied up. Start putting your vests on."

With the storm now looming over them, everyone started picking up their pace and scrambling to get things ready. Nate and Elizabeth finished getting the rope prepared and
started putting their life jackets on.

Nate took another swig from his flask, still looking out at the water. He could still spot a few fins drifting about, although who knew how many were hidden by the rough water, he wondered. He had been hoping the storm would have chased them off, but it was almost as if they knew about the upcoming opportunity for another meal.

Chapter Seven

The rain had started coming down at a steady downfall and the water had risen to a frightening level, submerging the sandy beaches and reaching the hull of the anchored dinghy. Three of the trees were now hosts to their temporary residents hanging on for dear life as the tall trunks bent and swayed in the wind.

Amber, Henry, Laura, and Elizabeth were perched on the sides of the trees, secured firmly to the trunks by the ropes and their iron grips. Elizabeth had her forehead pressed into the tree, eyes tightly shut and quietly muttering to herself.

Please let us make it through this, please let us make it through this, please, she
prayed.

She had already not been having a good trip. While everyone had been sharing the same fate, the circumstances had hit her the worst. She had been in shock for hours before Laura had eased her out of it the first time, just in time for Tim to be attacked, sending her back into a state of shock. It had been one thing to witness Captain Sterling being pulled into the water through a camera lens, but it was far worse to have a front row seat to the attack on her long-time cohort, someone she had spent more time with than with anyone else on the set.

Tim's savage death had shaken her to her core.

She had already been through a similar experience long before this one, and she kept replaying the event over and over in her head, still fresh in her mind, the overwhelming emotions layered on top of the present horror.

It had been a warm summer evening and Elizabeth had been combing the beach at New Smyrna, Florida, picking up seashells and snapping the occasional photo with her camera. The sun hung just above the horizon, glowing like a large golden coin and painting the sky in soft shades of orange and pink.

Next to her walked Noah, her fiancé, sporting a black and red, skin-tight wet suit and carrying a yellow surfboard at his side. He had short blonde hair that just covered his eyes.

They walked down the beach together, talking, laughing, and enjoying their time together.

"How about we go to L.A?" he asked her. "We can find a nice place right on the
beach, maybe walk to the pier on the weekends."

She scrunched her face up. "L.A? And go broke after two months of living there?
No thanks. What about Miami?" she countered.

"Miami? Miami is more expensive than L.A! And the summers there are worse, too."

"No they're not!"

"Yes they are."

"No they're not!"

"Guaranteed summer is one hundred times hotter in Miami than in L.A." Noah smiled at her and teasingly gave her a shove.

She laughed and shoved him back before taking hold of his hand. They continued in silence, happy to be together.

"Are you ready to turn around?" he finally asked.

She nodded, put her head on his shoulder for a moment and gave him a stifled

"Mhm." He kissed the top of her head and let go of her hand.

"Alright. Let me catch one more wave and we'll head back to our room."

He jogged off towards the water laughing as Elizabeth chased him to the water's edge.

"No, baby!" she cried. "Go later."

He turned and smiled before tossing his board into the water and climbing on top and paddling his way out into the ocean. She crossed her arms as he went further out.

Boys, she thought and kicked at the sand with her foot.

She watched him until he stopped paddling, sat up on his board, and scanned the waters searching for the perfect wave, just as he always had done. In the distance she could see him turn his head towards her, smiling, and he pointed in one direction across the water before he switched his hand into a thumbs up. He began paddling off in the direction he had pointed to where a wave began to form. As it got bigger, he pulled himself up and stood on his board, riding it.

Elizabeth couldn't help but smile. She loved this man with every fiber of her being. She would never admit it to him, but she even loved watching him surf. The way he would get into the zone, the way he'd skim his hand along the side of the wave, everything about his movements reminded her why she loved him so much. His loving, carefree, and relaxed way of living balanced perfectly with her own private, quiet, and cautious characteristics. She felt as if she had found the yin to her yang.

"Wooohooo!" she heard Noah shout off in the distance. He was picking up speed now, and found himself in the tunnel of the wave.

This was her favorite sight. She thought the way the water seemed to bend over and around him looked so…striking. The huge wave curved over him and crashed, the white foam of the sea splashing everywhere out in front of him.

Soon he was out of sight. All she could do now was slowly walk down the beach, unsure if he was still in the watery tunnel or if he had "wiped out," as he called it. She scanned the water, looking for a sign of him, until she spotted the thin, flat line of his
surfboard floating on the surface. But no fiancé.

She had seen this time and again, but it was always the part that made her the most nervous. The fear that one of these days he wouldn't resurface stuck in her mind, but, as always, his head popped up from under the surface with a big, toothy grin. She released a
gentle exhale.

He pumped his hand up in the air and cried another "Wooohooo!" before wiping his eyes and looking toward shore. Their eyes met.

Even at this distance, she felt her heart leap from their eye contact. He sure had a
way with her.

He suddenly dunked his head back under the water.

Now he's just messing with me, she thought to herself, although she really didn't
mind it.

His head came back up after a few seconds and he darted his face around, looking… confused. Then he went back under. Was he looking for something, she wondered, or just goofing on her more.

He didn't resurface. 20 seconds… 30 seconds… 40 seconds… until he finally came back up to the surface gasping for breath.

"Ah- uh- wha?!" was all he could seem to get out with his arms flailing around,
searching for something to grab onto.

He found his board and tried to hoist himself up onto it, but before he could
stabilize himself on it, he slipped back under the water.

No, he was pulled back under, Elizabeth realized.

She stared in confusion that quickly grew into concern. What was going on? He'd
never had trouble in the water like this before.

Then she saw it.

A dark gray fin emerged from the water, only to disappear as quickly as it had appeared. Noah came back up from the water in a frenzy, splashing against the waves and
screaming, "Help! Elizabeth!"

He was pulled back under and Elizabeth panicked.

"Noah!" Her hands cupped her mouth in shock and she started screaming for help, but there was no one around.

Noah resurfaced again and the gray fin reappeared next to him.

"Elizabeth!" he shouted.

The gray fin rose out of the water until a large, dark mass came up underneath it and engulfed him. It was a huge shark, and hungry. It latched its jaws onto Noah's waist and started thrashing him around in a violent commotion of water.

"Elizabeth! Elizabeth!" he cried.

She watched in horror as he called for her, unable to do anything.

She heard someone calling.

"Elizabeth! Elizabeth! You okay, honey?"

She snapped back to reality. She looked around, still perched on her tree, and looked over at Laura.

Laura smiled. "Hey, hun. Are you with us?" she asked.

Elizabeth nodded quietly. It had been a long while since she'd been pulled back to that day. She couldn't say anything as she worked on coming back to the present.

"We're going to be okay now," Amber piped in. "Gage said once the storm passes, the sharks will likely move on as long as they don't have anything else to eat. He said they'll look for food elsewhere and we will be safe to head back to the yacht."

She was in the next tree, the largest of the six, and was grasping the tree, right next to Henry. He was gripping the tree with all his strength, his eyes shut tightly, as he muttered to himself quietly.

Elizabeth looked around her. Nate, Gage, and Eric were in their trees, and, of course, of the seven of them Nate seemed the most relaxed. He stood on the makeshift rungs that stuck out from his tree, his hands behind his head, leaning back against the rope that held him to the tree. He still had his shades on even though the clouds had blocked out any remaining sunshine, and once again it looked to Elizabeth like he could have been asleep.

She had no idea how he could be so relaxed hanging in a tree during a cyclone with sharks nearby who hungered for another human meal after having eaten the captain, the cook, and their director. She was convinced that nothing could shake him and she was
envious that he could take trauma head on like that and still be able to hold his head high.

Nate was awake, but his mind was racing even though he didn't show it. He couldn't help but wonder what was going to happen to them next. They had already lost three members in their group in a matter of what? A day? Not even? Did they really have a chance? What would happen if he were gobbled up by another huge shark? What would he
be leaving behind?

He realized these last many years he had spent either high or drunk, sometimes both. What about Laura? His mind focused on his wife. Would she even miss him? Maybe not.

He quietly gasped. That thought hit him hard, harder than he would have expected.

He reached into his pocket for his flask and grasped it, but hesitated. Maybe he shouldn't take a swig right at that moment. He was hiding up in a tree for his life, after all. His empty hand retreated from his pocket.

Minutes passed. Then an hour. Then two hours, then three. The storm was on top of them now. Everyone was wet, cold, and tired.

Eric was shifting on his wooden rungs, struggling to stay comfortable. He looked around the now submerged island. Their gear and equipment were in the clutches of the ocean. The coolers of food had started to float, carried away by the intense tides. The chuck box was heavy enough to stay anchored in the sand. At least, for now, Eric thought. But their tents, although packed up, were long gone. They had been the first things to be carried off.

He really hoped they didn't have to spend another night there. He wasn't so sure he could stand another one. At least they hadn't seen any sign of the sharks in a while. Maybe they really did swim off in search of an easier meal. If so, all he had to do now was wait out the storm.

One of his foot-rungs suddenly gave out from being pummeled by the wind and the rain for so long and it fell into the chaotic waters below him. He caught himself against the bark of the tree before he fell and he tried to move his now freely hanging leg to the other rung. Awkwardly, he stood on the one rung with both of his feet on it now. He barely had enough room to hold both comfortably and his grip strengthened around the tree as the adrenaline shot through his body.

He became even more frightened as he alerted himself to the increasing danger of
their…no, of his situation.

He was the only one struggling to stay on his tree. He looked at Gage, who clung to his own tree, and was now shouting something to him, although he could only hear a faint voice within the roar of the wind, rain, and waves crashing against what remained of the island.

"What??" he shouted back.

He hoped for a brief pause in the noise to hear what Gage was saying, but he had no such luck. He looked across at the others.

Gage had been the only one who even noticed that Eric was struggling. Henry and Amber buried their faces against their tree. Laura had a determined look to her, even with her eyes closed, but her face was calm. Eric thought it was if she somehow knew she was going to make it out. Elizabeth was motionless, the side of her face pressed against the tree looking off in the other direction.

Then his eyes landed on Nate, who stared back at him. Like Laura, he looked calm, but he had a more serious look in his eyes, a look, Eric thought, which seemed to urge Eric to persevere and let him know that he could make it. Throughout their trip, not once had he seen Nate take anything seriously. Until now. Eric felt a hint of reassurance.

I can do this, Eric thought to himself. I've been trained for this, Sort of. I just have to keep holding on. My life is at stake. This adrenaline coursing through my veins is going to help me make it out alive. He kept repeating these thoughts, encouraging himself and reminding himself that he had what it took to survive.

As he kept reciting these mantras, a new look of determination took over his face, and Gage saw it. Even through the intense wind and rain, Gage could see the sheer burst of willpower spread throughout Eric's body. From his now firm, clenching grip around the tree and the locked focus of his eyes, Gage knew Eric was not going to go down without a fight.

Then Eric's other foothold gave away.

Gage watched in horror as the body of his second in command jerked and slipped slightly down the trunk of the tree. The only thing that was keeping Eric from plunging into the violent waves below was the rope around his waist and the bear hug he used to press his body against the tree.

The brief look of determination and willpower was quickly replaced by one of panic. His legs writhed about as he tried to regain his composure. Finally he was able to wrap his legs around the tree and hold on with them, too, but he was still struggling. He was strong, but Gage knew he couldn't stay like this for too much longer.

Gage continued to watch as his second-mate clung to the tree with all the strength he could go into his arms and legs.

"Just…just hold on!" Gage shouted over, but he knew there was no point in saying it. The wind and the waves were too loud for anything to be audible, and he also could see Eric ever so slowly sliding down the tree as his muscles began to give out.

Erics' face showed an uneasy mix of terror, shock, and resolve. Then, all at once, he slid another two feet further down the trunk of the tree, but he was still bound to it by the
rope.

Gage realized that at least Eric wouldn't slide out from under the rope as the girth of the tree below him was wider than the middle and top, where he had started. The more he slid down the tree, the tighter the rope would hold him.

Eric realized that too. After the last terrifying slide down those few feet, he now tried nudging himself down further to no avail. Eric was held against the tree even more firmly than before, although now he was so close to the sea beneath him that he was constantly being splashed by the waves. At times his legs would be half submerged in the salty water.

Eric looked over and up at Gage and started to say something, but he changed his
mind and opted for a simple thumbs up and a nervous smile.

Gage smiled back and nodded.

Things were going to be okay, Gage thought. Eric had worked something out, and though uncomfortable, he was at least still safe. Gage looked over the rest of the survivors.

None of them seemed to be having any trouble with their footholds.

Suddenly Gage heard a single loud, horrifying shriek pierce through the intense roar of the storm.

He looked back down at Eric and saw a large gray mass circling him in the chaotic
water. Eric was using his legs to kick at the creature in an attempt to steer it away from him.

The creature then circled back around and Eric went for another kick with both his feet, but the beast surfaced with its maw wide open and clamped it around his leg. The shark started thrashing its head back and forth in the water, pulling on Eric's legs and trying to ensure its next meal was his.

Eric screamed in pain as it inched itself up his leg and bit down on his thigh. Gage
watched in horror as the shark disappeared into the dark abyss, taking Eric's leg with it.
Eric stared down at his bleeding stump, paralyzed in shock, and Gage saw his body go limp, the stress and fear too much for him.

Gage knew he had to do something. He couldn't let his friend die, not without trying to save him. He reached for the knife in his pocket

and started slicing his own ropes. He cut through one, then another, and as he cut the third, the rest went slack and he slipped down and his feet landed on the next rungs down that he had first hammered into the tree. Salty water splashed violently around his legs. He tucked the knife away. Okay, he thought, if I can just make the jump to Eric's tree, maybe I can help pull
him back up.

He carefully shimmied his way around the tree and put both of his feet on one foot rung. It shifted under his weight, but it remained stuck in its groove in the tree. He looked
over at Eric's tree and he closed his eyes for a second, mentally preparing himself.

He jumped.

He slammed into the trunk of the tree right above Eric's limp body and latched on to it with all his strength. He looked up at the other survivors and saw them all watching him in awe.

"Okay, one obstacle down," he said to himself.

He looked down at Erics' motionless body on the tree, the waves crashing into him and throwing his free limbs around. Gage carefully began descending down the tree when he saw that their brief respite from the sharks was over.

A large gray fin emerged from the water. It was followed by another and then
another.

Damn it, he thought. *The blood from Eric's leg must have attracted them.*

One of the sharks latched onto Eric's other leg, dangling above it, and wrestled away with it in his mouth. A surge of adrenaline shot through Eric and his eyes shot open as he let out another horrifying scream.

With one hand still clutching onto the tree, Eric used his other to repeatedly bash the shark on its snout, furiously trying to break its grip on his remaining leg.

It was no use. The shark tore away his other leg and darted away.

As the blood began pouring out of Eric's second stump, the other sharks swam in for their own prizes and began nibbling and biting and tearing away at the helpless body tied to the tree.

One chomped onto his arm as Eric flailed about and, with enough force, managed to pull Eric up and out from the rope and disappeared into a sloshing of frantic gray masses and crashing waves.

Gage yelled out. He couldn't do anything from where he was and he just watched as another cohort was taken away. Not only had Eric been his second-mate, but had grown to be Gage's good friend in the time they had served under Captain Sterling together.

Gage pressed his face into the tree bark and broke down. He cried. It was all too much for him. He had been trying so hard to save his crew, but one by one he just kept
losing them. And now his friend.

He opened his eyes to the scene below. There were fewer fins now and the missing sharks were presumably enjoying their latest snack. The ones that remained waited patiently for whoever might fall next like a fleshy fruit from the tree.

Gage's face felt numb. He was wet and cold, and he could barely see anything between the intense wind and the rain and tears in his eyes. Even the others on their trees
weren't much more than fuzzy figures.

He couldn't think. He didn't know what to do. He didn't know for how much longer he could hang on, or if he really even wanted to anymore, for that matter. He was getting weaker by the minute from the shear strain he had been putting on his arms and legs to hang on. At least if he fell, he was on the tree that had the last dinghy tied up to it. Maybe he could aim for it and break his fall.

Or maybe he shouldn't aim for it and just let the crazy waters consume his fate. He wasn't sure yet.

As he stared at the dinghy, disassociating, he saw the last fins in the water suddenly dart away from his tree. Did someone else fall? Did he lose another soul due to his failure as a first mate?

He squinted around at the others and did a head count; one, two-three, four, five… nope. They were all still alive and they had all their limbs. He looked past them into the
seemingly endless horizon of tall, roaring waves. He saw… something.

There was some kind of commotion in the water not in sync with the commotion of the storm. It looked like a series of splashes, as if a stone was skipping across the surface of a pond, a very chaotic and unpleasant pond.

If Hell had not already broken loose, it was now on a rampage and tearing up the ocean. Breaking through the already violent waves a series of thrashes began beneath the tired survivors. No one could tell what was going on.

The sharks were still there with various fins protruding from the water, but were they fighting each other now, Gage wondered. Were there so many sharks that they began
competing for who was going to get the next tasty treat that fell from the trees?

The realization hit Gage like a gust of the cyclone. This was it. This was their chance.

His mind kicked into high gear and he waved at the rest of the group to get their attention.

They had also noticed the disturbance in the water below, or at least the increased disturbance.

He caught Nate's eye first, who pulled his sunglasses down slightly and nodded. Gage slowly pointed around to everyone in the trees and then to the dinghy down below before pointing to the top of his wrist and mouthed NOW. Henry looked startled, but the
others seemed to have gotten Gage's message.

"We're leaving NOW".

Gage pulled his knife back out from his pocket and made a tossing motion towards Nate, who nodded again and prepared himself. Gage tossed the blade towards him and he
was just able to catch it by the blade. He let out an inaudible sigh of relief and started cutting through the rope that held him up.

Gage started to shimmy carefully down the tree towards the dinghy. It might have been anchored to the tree, but it was far from stationary. It thrashed about on the waves like it was a toy in the bathtub of an energetic child. It was a wonder to Gage that it hadn't filled up with water at this point.

Gage got down to the base of the tree and the cold and violent waves crashed up against his back. He stretched his leg out in an attempt to pull the dinghy towards him.

Almost... got it, he thought to himself.

As his foot touched the rubber, the waves slammed into his back again and knocked his lower half completely off the tree. He hung there, his arms clenched around the tree with his waist submerged in the roaring waters. He could feel the sandy beach right under his feet, but he dare not let go. If he did, he knew he would have no control over where the water would take him.

First things first, he knew. Get out of the shark infested water. It was difficult to pull his legs up and out of the strong motion of the water, but after a few tries, he managed to re-wrap himself around the tree. Now to try for the dinghy. Again.

Gage waited and watched the little boat toss around on the surface of the waves and tried to time his shot perfectly. He looked up at the others who were all helping each other by passing the knife around so they could cut loose their bindings. Nate was standing on his footholds, now untied, waiting for his next order from Gage. Laura cut herself loose from the ropes and reached out to hand the knife to Elizabeth, who took the blade and started cutting her ropes.

Gage looked back at the boat floating underneath. He focused and stared at the raft
as it shifted back and forth, here and there until… now!

He thrust his leg against the raft as it was pushed towards him and he latched on with all his might, his ankle over the side, until he successfully got control over it. He threw his second leg in, pulled the dinghy toward him, and after regaining his composure, he released and fell into the dinghy.

Gage had to act fast to get the dinghy ready to go. He got to the engine and started working with the controls, trying to get it started. It normally didn't take much more than a flip of a couple of switches to get it going, but the rain and the horrible lighting was making it difficult.

Elizabeth had set herself free and had handed the knife over to Amber, who started hacking away. Laura climbed down her tree and waited, eyeing the dinghy. Nate and Elizabeth soon followed.

A new sound broke through the storm. The engine had finally started, and Gage collapsed in relief for just a moment. Laura leaped from her tree and landed squarely in the middle of the boat. Gage hadn't realized just how athletic she was, although it made sense to him as she had done all her own stunts in their film.

With the engine now running, Gage grabbed the back-up collapsible oar from the compartment underneath the seats. He put it together and used it to reach out and get hold of the other trees, pulling the boat closer to them.

After a few tries he managed to pull the dinghy closer to the trees that still held Nate and Elizabeth and they lumbered down carefully and piled into the boat. Now all Gage had to collect Amber and Henry.

All around them the commotion in the water had increased. It was hard to tell which way was what with so much violent spray in the air at once.

"What's going on?" Laura yelled over the storm to Gage.

Without taking his eyes off the next tree, he yelled back, "We're going back to the yacht!"

He hooked the oar against the side of Amber and Henrys' tree and pulled. Slowly, using the oar's leverage to inch closer and closer, he pulled and pushed until…their dinghy stopped moving.

He looked back at the rope that anchored the dinghy, now taut and extended to its
furthest length. There were still five more feet between them and the tree.

Amber had cut herself free and was helping Henry get loose from his ropes. It was no easy task for her to cut the thick ropes in the intense weather and with very limited light. Her hand was too sore to continue, and she gave the knife to Henry who took over cutting himself free.

Amber looked below, almost quizzically, at the small boat and her crew-mates. It looked like they were having trouble getting any closer to them, but why, of all times, were they making a break for it now?

The sharks didn't seem to have disappeared, although they did appear to be
preoccupied by something else. *What*, she wondered…*and in the middle of this storm?*

The yacht crew had already learned the hard way that these dinghies were no match for a hungry shark, and there were still several swimming around them.

Whatever, Amber thought to herself. She was tired, sore, and "so over it" now that she didn't have the energy to be afraid anymore. She snatched the knife back from Henry, who had already become visibly tired from trying to cut the rope. Amber started sawing away at it with a renewed vigor. Only seconds later it finally gave away and fell down into the crazy water below.

Good, Amber thought, *now that that was done... what next?*

Gage was struggling to get the boat closer to the tree and Laura stood and motioned for Amber and Henry to jump in.

Amber nodded and mentally and physically prepared herself. Henry was having second thoughts. She placed her hand on his shoulder and looked into his eyes and he looked back and in mere seconds they had carried on an entire conversation that boiled
down to her telling him, "You can do this. Let's get out of here."

Amber slowly shimmied down the tree, doing her best not to accidentally nudge Henry off, and reached out towards the boat as Laura extended her hand. The violent rocking and swaying of the boat made it almost impossible for them to make contact and
one lurch of the boat almost threw Laura off into the water.

Amber adjusted her position, getting just a little bit lower, and reached out again. This time, she was just able to reach Laura's straining hand and she grabbed it. She almost pulled Laura out of the boat a second time, but Laura stayed strong. Amber closed her eyes and leaped.

With Laura's help, instead of slamming against the side of the dinghy, Amber at least was able to get her upper half inside the boat with her legs frantically kicking over the edge. Nate and Laura each grabbed an arm and hoisted her all the way in and she lay there prone for a second before sitting up, dazed.

She had made it, she realized with tears in her eyes.. But now it was Henry's turn.

Henry stared down at the dinghy. He was petrified. He couldn't move. How was he going to make that jump? He didn't have the actors' experience of being able to move and jump around on command, like Nate, Amber, and Laura had. Shoot, even being the cinematographer, Elizabeth had the strength to hold her own just from lugging around the heavy cameras and film equipment all day. But he was just the assistant director. The most he ever carried around all day was a clipboard and the occasional coffee tray for the crew.

Amber motioned for him to come down, waving her arms and shouting. He couldn't tell what she was saying, but he figured it was something encouraging. She had been very supportive this whole trip, and surprisingly, very collected after everything that had happened.

On the surface she had seemed to Henry like your everyday "young and privileged" girl who never had anything go wrong for her. Like me, he thought. But there was more to her, and Henry felt like he had only just barely scratched the surface of her story.

Maybe…he thought.

After finally building up his courage, and unable to stand the thought of being the burden that dragged the group down any longer, he slowly started inching his way down the tree.

The gap between the dinghy and the tree appeared to him to get wider as he got lower. How could that be? Panic started setting in, but he looked back at Amber who, through the chaos of the storm and the sharks, gave him a quiet look of reassurance and
held out her hand.

Everything seemed to slow down for Henry. The world went quiet. All that existed for Henry at that moment was he and Amber as they stared into each other's eyes. It was all that mattered. He could do this.

Without any other distraction, he jumped.

Chapter Eight

Nate stood at the bow of the Sail Happy, staring off at the horizon. They had finally sailed out of the heaviest part of the storm, although it was still raining and the entire deck was wet and submerged in about an inch of water. The drain system on the ship was not meant for taking on so much water, but it was at the very least
still working.

Half of the sun chairs on the ship were scattered across the deck. The other half were missing completely. Everything was a mess, but Nate couldn't be more relieved. Or devastated. Or numb. Or… well, he was dealing with a variety of emotions now. But he was alive and on his way home.

His gaze shifted to the dinghy hanging off the side of the ship. It was in rough shape. Most of its supplies were missing, probably resting on the seafloor at this point. The engine was gone, too, but the most obvious damage to the little boat was the giant bite mark that scarred the rubber exterior. It was completely deflated.

He shuddered, remembering the events that had unfolded only an hour before. He'd been in the Hollywood business for years, acting in suspenseful horror movies, action packed thrillers, and heart-wrenching dramas. But this one morning, no…this entire simple camping trip…turned out to be the most intense time of his life.
Nearly half of the people he'd started this outing with were now dead, and the others
were trying to pull themselves together.

He had been doing alright for most of the weekend. Even after losing their captain, with whom he had forged a strong bond, and Tim, the director of a handful of movies he'd starred in, he'd managed to keep a level head. Being an actor meant putting yourself in extraordinary situations, and although they were fabricated situations, they were still scenarios that he had to put himself in, with both mind and body.

Acting had a way of desensitizing you that way after a while, he had realized.

But being up close and in real life action, with no stunt doubles, no retakes, no safety measures or even snack breaks, that was what he'd just gone through, actual in-your-face
danger and bodily harm and loss.

It had shaken Nate, completely. Even for him, he knew, with his normally laid-back demeanor, it was going to take some time to get out of this funk.

He was having a hard time letting go of what had transpired. The past is in the past, after all, he said to himself, but you don't forget something like this so easily…and boy, did he want to forget.

He stared at the bite mark in the side of the dinghy as the events that had unfolded replayed over and over in his head.

* * *

Gage had cut the rope that anchored the dinghy to the tree the moment he saw
Henry jumped. He wanted to make sure that they departed as soon as possible. He wasn't sure how much time they had to leave the island, and he knew he needed every second he could get.

He didn't waste any time untying the anchor or pulling the rope back in or even
checking to see if Henry had made it onto the boat. He revved the engine, and they were off.

Finally he realized that something was wrong. Amber and Elizabeth were both
screaming and hanging off the side of the boat. Henry was nowhere to be seen.
Laura turned towards Gage and shouted. He couldn't hear her over the sound of the
engine, much less the storm, but he could read her lips.

"STOP!"

He hesitated, but slowed the dinghy to a stop and moved up to join the others.

"What happened?" he yelled.

He looked over the side to see… nothing. No Henry. No sharks. Yet. "Where is he?" he yelled again at Amber. "I thought you helped him down?" Amber shook her head, her eyes wide with panic.

"He didn't make it onto the boat! He fell into the water and I don't know where he
is!"

Gage put his hands behind his head and turned back towards the engine. He had lost another soul to the horrors of the ocean, and this time he knew it was his fault. He hadn't been able to help the others getting mauled by the sharks, but he could have waited…even just another second…before cutting the anchor and taking off. He should have waited, he knew.

What do I do now? he thought to himself. *If Henry's out in the water in this weather with all of these sharks around, he's as good as…*

He looked out into the night and saw…something. It wasn't much, especially given the circumstances, but it was something. A small splash of water off in the distance behind the dinghy. It was too small to be a shark.

For a brief moment a head popped up above the tall waves. It was Henry.

He reached his hand out in a motion like that of a doggy paddle, but not in the water. Gage didn't think it looked like he was waving to them, either, but it was more like… he was telling them to leave? Did he want them to go without him?

Henry's hand dipped below the water once again and then his other hand rose above the waves with something in his grip. It was the rope! Before Gage had taken off, he had been able to grab hold of the rope that had anchored the dinghy to the tree!

Gage smiled and even let out a relieved laugh. This guy was tougher than he put on, and maybe even he didn't know it!

Gage turned towards the others with a smile and pointed at Henry out in the waves. They looked at where Gage was pointing, and in a matter of seconds Amber's face morphed from panic to relief, and then to horror.

Gage turned around to see Henry waiting for them to speed off again, only this time he saw the reality of the situation. A large gray fin protruded from the water only a few meters behind Henry. It was closing in on him, getting ready for a meal.

Gage screamed and immediately gunned the engine, knocking everyone onto their butts and nearly throwing Nate off the boat entirely.

The dinghy skipped across the waves as they made their way towards the yacht off in the distance. Water splashed into the dinghy, spraying everyone and keeping them from getting their footing, but Gage kept the throttle as full as he dared in the turbulent water.

He kept looking back at Henry to make sure he was still with them. He was, but the

The shark fin was still closing in. They weren't going fast enough. They needed more speed.

In a split second Gage made the decision to go full throttle, a risk in itself because of the waves but also because it could flood and kill the engine.

Gage needed to save Henry. He couldn't lose another life, not if he could help it.

Amber climbed to the back of the boat and dipped her hands into the water behind them in search of the rope. She found it and started pulling it out of the water in the hope of getting Henry closer to the boat and further from the shark still gaining on him. Every foot helped, she knew.

Nate joined her and together they took turns pulling Henry in. Laura sat in the front, trying to stay out of their way. Any more people back there and things would get too crowded and becoming counterproductive, she knew.

She watched as her husband and Amber attempted to help save Henry. She couldn't help but admire Nate. Well, she admired Amber too for what they were doing, but she had not expected Nate to be one to jump in to the rescue. He was actually feeling… feelings, she thought. Whether the feeling was courage or fear, that was new to her. Or, at the very least,

It had been too long since she'd seen this side of him.

The four of them watched the yacht slowly grow in size as they neared it, and Gage felt increased hope that they could make it. They had to make it. The ship was close enough that he could now see it rockin in the storm. It must have taken on a lot of water in the cyclone, he realized, and he could only hope the drain system could handle it, at least until he got there to get things bailed out.

Amber and Nate kept pulling Henry in closer to the boat, but the strain of pulling a human against the waves in a speeding boat and in a cyclone was exhausting them both. Amber finally collapsed back and let go of the rope, but Nate kept pulling on the rope with everything he had.

Henry was only a few meters away from the boat now. Behind him was the shark, now joined by two more fins. The commotion they were causing started to attract more
sharks as the feeding frenzy spread between them all.

Henry held on tightly to the rope. He saw Amber had gotten too tired to continue pulling him in, and he started to do his share and help pull himself closer, hand over hand with the rope. He was not going to be a helpless burden to anyone again. They were trying to save him and all he had been doing was holding on. It was time to pull his own weight, literally.

It was difficult pulling himself towards the boat as it sped along the roaring waves slapping him against the surface of the water time after time. The adrenaline coursing through his body helped him persevere and ever so slowly he made his way closer to the
dinghy.

He saw Nate and Amber at the back of the boat, both now too tired to continue pulling him in. They were simply holding on to the rope. He was so close.

He started to believe that he could finally get himself to safety, but then he felt the
excruciatingly sharp pain shot up his leg.

Amber watched in horror as one of the sharks reached him and clamped onto his leg. She heard him let out a loud scream, instantly to be muffled and drowned out by the water that entered his lungs.

"Henry!" she cried out.

The dinghy slowed down dramatically with the sudden anchoring effect of the
weight of the shark.

Gage turned to see what had happened, but he didn't slow down. They were so close to the yacht, he couldn't stop now.

Amber leaned over the edge of the boat and shouted out to Henry, "Just hang on!
We're almost back on the ship!"

He couldn't hear her.

All he heard was the water filling his ears over and over again as he kept submerging with the weight of the shark. The pain was so bad, but he tried to keep himself from blacking out, knowing that if he lost consciousness, that would be it. He'd be done and there would be no saving him.

Knowing this terrified him but also encouraged him, and he tightened his grip on the rope until it started digging into his skin. It hurt, but the dozens of shark teeth on his leg still hurt more and masked the pain of the rope on his palms.

Nate stood at the back of the dinghy clutching the rope. He looked behind him to see how close they were to the yacht and he was just able to make out the ladder built into the starboard side. It was their salvation from this nightmare, but Henry was still in trouble.

"Laura!" Nate shouted.

He looked at her and met her fixed gaze, breaking her from her trance of looking at… him. She moved back in the dinghy and joined him at his side. He nodded towards the rope as if to tell her to grab on. She was the only one he could trust to keep the rope from slipping further out. He knew she took her workouts very seriously.

She latched on, wrapped the excess rope around her arms, and held on. Her arm muscles bulged as she took on her task, allowing Nate to let go. His arms were limp with
exhaustion.

Amber grabbed the section of rope he dropped in alarm and wondered why he
would let it go in the first place.

Nate left Henry's fate in the women's hands for a moment and dug around the dinghy in search of something to help them. He needed a tool to do the unthinkable. He
scrounged the boat top to bottom but came up with nothing.

He looked back at Henry. It didn't look like he was going to hold on much longer,
and they were almost back at the yacht. Nate knew what he needed.

Elizabeth sat in her corner of the dinghy, too worn out to be much help to anyone, but she was reading the situation like a book. She watched Nate tear apart the whole dinghy \and she realized what he needed.

"Hey!" she shouted to him.

He looked back at her with a stressed look in his eyes that she had never seen before. She reached into her back pocket and pulled out a small red trinket, a Swiss army knife. She found it to be a handy tool to always have on her. She tossed it to him.

He barely caught it in both hands. He looked at the tool and then back at her.

Neither said a word, but she knew what he planned, and he knew she knew.

He nodded at her and extended the blade of the tool, analyzing it, before he returned to the back of the boat where the others still held on tightly to the thick rope.

Amber saw the blade in his hand. Her eyes widened. Laura was doing the brunt of
the work, and keeping one hand on the rope, Amber used her other to push Nate back.

"Don't!" She cried. "Stop!"

He looked at her and she saw the intention in his eyes.

"I have to," he shouted back.

She tried to push him back again, but she was so fatigued she couldn't hold him off for a long time.

Confused, Laura watched Amber fend off Nate. What was going on? What was Nate doing that had Amber pushing against him? Laura looked away from the rope for a second to see the open knife in Nate's hand.

Shocked, she screamed at him, "What the hell are you doing? You can't cut the rope! You'll kill him!"

He looked at her, inched over to her side and put his empty hand around her waist. He leaned in close to her ear.

"I know," he said softly.

She pulled away and looked into his eyes to try to read just what kind of plan he was hatching.

Nate pulled her in for a kiss. Their lips met and everything went quiet. They were lost together in their kiss, the world going to hell around them. Their eyes closed, and Laura embraced the kiss, letting go of the rope in the process.

The dinghy lurched forward for a second as it now had distance between it and the
shark, but its movement forward was shunted again as the rope went taut.

Laura broke away from Nate and reached back down into the water for the rope, but before she could grab it, Nate launched himself over the side of the dinghy and into the depths below.

She moved back, stunned at her husband throwing himself into the ocean in the middle of a shark-infested cyclone. She leaned forward and squinted at the water. There was no sign of him.

An arm emerged from the water behind the shark and came down onto its shiny wet skin like a hammer striking an anvil. The blade of the pocketknife sunk into the beast's spine. Immediately the animal started thrashing around and it let go of Henry's crushed leg.

Nate grabbed onto the rope and held on, joining Henry in the torture of being
dragged behind the boat in the ice-cold water.

He knew he had successfully "surgically" removed the shark from the situation, at least for now, and it was just in time. The silhouette of the yacht now loomed over them and the dinghy slowed to a stop.

Nate knew they were almost safe. All they had to do was climb the ladder. He tried to throw the pocketknife back into the dinghy, but missed. He watched as it bounced off the side and into the water, never to be seen again. Whatever, he thought. Elizabeth could
always buy another. Heck, he'd buy her one himself.

It was time to climb to safety.

He started pulling himself towards the dinghy and grabbed Henry by his waist and started lugging him towards the dinghy. Henry helped him climb the rope now that Nate
could only use one arm and together, they started to pull themselves into the little boat.

Gage and Laura reached down into the water to help them up and Nate let them grab Henry first. He let go and started paddling in the water, waiting for his turn. Elizabeth
was already climbing up the ladder of the yacht.

Gage then followed behind her after grabbing Henry, now hanging around his torso and making the climb a slow and difficult one.

Laura reached down and pulled Nate out of the water with one hand. They waited together, looking at each other with relief, while Amber started her climb. Knowing they were safe, they lowered their guard and embraced each other once again. They held each
others close, neither wanting to let go.

"I love you," Nate whispered in her ear. He didn't know why he said it, but he knew he wanted to. It felt right.

Laura held him tightly and nodded, too stunned to respond.

Suddenly the two of them were violently knocked off their feet and fell back into the dinghy. A loud bursting sound erupted around them and the dinghy started to tilt.

With the back of the dinghy between its large teeth, the large shark that had clamped onto Henry's leg only moments before tugged at the little dinghy. Nate knew it was the same shark. It was still bleeding from his wound in its back.

Its jaws quickly destroyed the back of the hull and the boat started flooding with
water. They only had seconds before it would be completely submerged.

As the dinghy took on more water, it tilted even more steeply and Nate and Laura started sliding toward the back of the boat towards the enormous maw that awaited them.

The thrashing shark was mad, hungry, and only a few feet away from getting its next meal.

Nate began kicking the beast in its snout to get it to retreat, and Laura joined in.

"Go to hell!" she yelled at it.

The shark was determined to feed and it held onto the back of the dinghy with its
jaws while it continued to try to crush it.

More fins suddenly appeared in the water around them, waiting for their own chance to join in the feeding. Nate and Laura were surrounded and soon they would be floating in the roiling water around them.

"Nate!" Laura called out, panicked now and doing everything she could to move
back up to the highest part of the sinking boat.

"What?" he called back.

She pulled on his free hand and then held it tight, locking eyes with him.

"I love you, too," she said in a shaky voice.

He stared at her, wondering how they had ever gotten so distant in the first place. He now saw what he loved about her, her determination in the face of poor odds, her ability to stay level-headed at the worst of times, and her breathtakingly beautiful, steely gray eyes.

He tightened his grip on her hand and looked at her reassuringly, as if he thought he could still find them a way out of their situation, although truthfully, he had no idea what to do next.

They looked back at the immediate danger crunching away below them and braced
themselves for the worst. This could be it, and for all they knew, it was.

But it wasn't.

At that moment a shape erupted mightily through the surface of the waves to their left in an incredible trajectory and it slammed into the shark chewing its way through the back of the dinghy. The impact caused it to release its grip on the dinghy and what was left of the little boat slapped down onto the water.

Nate and Laura stared in disbelief at their hidden savior, a large, sleek, dark gray
dolphin.

It now rose majestically back out of the water and then all hell broke loose once
again.

Shark fins darted around the water around them as other dolphins began erupting
out of the water and slamming back down on the predators.

They were attacking the sharks.

The boat began to sink fully into the water, and Nate and Laura were snapped out of staring at the dolphins as the large metal clamp at the end of a rope fell down from the deck of the yacht and landed on Nate's head.

"Ow! What the hell?!"

He rubbed his head and looked up to see Gage peering at him over the edge of the
yacht.

"Sorry! Latch on and I'll reel you two up!"

Nate grabbed the clamp and hooked it onto the front brace on the dinghy. Gage started winding up the rope with the crank system and slowly raising the dinghy bow first out of the water. Nate and Laura held on to the side of the boat as it ascended up the side of the yacht.

Chaos continued all around them. Dolphins leapt out of the air and back into the water and onto their prey. Sharks darted around through the waves, thrashing about and trying to successfully latch onto their porpoise attackers.

Tall waves crashed and slammed into the side of the yacht and the cyclone's rain
came down again like bullets from the heavens.

Nate and Laura were rising through the middle of it all.

Nate thought that it was almost, in a weird and mortifying sort of way, romantic.

Laura recognized his smug smile and they looked at each other and laughed.

Laura rested her head on his chest as they rose up together through the rain and the wind toward the deck of the yacht.

* * *

Nate broke free from the trance of recent memory and pulled his gaze away from the bite mark in the dinghy. He was long overdue for a nap, he decided, when Laura
approached him from behind and hugged him.

"You okay?" she asked him.

He breathed a deep sigh of relief as he felt her arms encircle him from behind.

"Yeah," he eventually responded. "Yeah, I guess I'll be alright."

He kept gazing out at the horizon and minutes passed before he spoke again.

"I need a drink," he said flatly.

Laura chuckled and rolled her eyes behind him.

Nate pulled her around and placed his hands over hers and then embracing her with his own hug. They looked at each other, entrusted to each other's arms.

Nate was still staring into her eyes when he heard a movement from the corner of
his deck. It was Gage emerging from below.

"Hey, man. How is everyone holding up?" Nate called out to him.

Gage walked over with a tired smile.

"Not bad. The skinny guy…"

"Henry?"

"Yes, Henry," Gage continued, "is going to make it. His leg isn't too pretty, but I have it splinted and wrapped, and I gave him some painkillers. He's out like a light right
Now, and so are the other two. They've… we've all been through a lot."
Nate closed his eyes as Laura rested her head against his chest.

"Yeah, understatement of the year."

He opened his eyes and looked at the first mate again.

"So, what the hell, dolphins saved us? Is that a thing?"

Gage smiled and walked over to the side of the ship. It was his moment to stare out at the sea.

Nate turned and saw, bouncing out of the water beside the yacht, were half a dozen dolphins, following them and making a series of clicking sounds. Laura thought it was as if they were dancing along beside them, and occasionally one would jump out of the water high enough to nearly reach her.

"No," Gage finally broke the silence as they marveled at the show in front of them. "It's not a thing. Not really. In fact, I didn't know it could even happen until a couple days ago." He turned around and leaned back on the railing and allowed his body to relax. "When we were on our way to the island, the captain and I heard someone broadcasting over the radio that he had spotted a shiver, a group of sharks that had just fed on a few juvenile dolphins. It's not irregular for sharks to eat a baby dolphin, but there's a big difference between a shark eating a dolphin and a bunch of sharks eating a bunch of baby dolphins. The parents, the mothers in particular, are not too happy with that."

Nate and Laura stood there, waiting for him to continue, while he pulled his knife
out of his pocket and started fidgeting with it, flipping it open and then closing it repeatedly.

"In fact," he finally went on, composed again, "according to Captain Sterling, something like this happened during his time out at sea years ago. The dolphins were so upset that they followed the sharks and then kept attacking them until there were floating bits of fresh meat from both sides all across the waves. I guess it was a pretty bloody
time..."

He trailed off with his words again as he remembered the gruesome story the late
the captain had told him.

"So," Nate picked up, "they weren't so much saving us as they were enacting a
horrible vengeance for their slain young. That's sweet."

Gage looked at him and smiled.

"That's what I said to the captain, too." He moved the railing and stretched once. "Hey, I've got to make sure the ship is going to keep running for our return trip. You two
ought to make like the others and catch some z's."

He pointed at them, punctuating with a finger, in a half-serious manner as walked
away and disappeared through a door into the hold of the ship.

Nate let go of Laura and took her hand. They both turned to look back out at the
ocean and the friendly, revenge-seeking creatures that continued to put on a show for them.

"You're going to come lay down, babe?" Laura asked. "He's right. It's been a while since we were able to get some sleep."

"Yeah…" Nate started to say more, but stopped. She looked at him, concerned.

"You okay? What's wrong?" she asked. "I mean, besides this entire weekend. Do you want to talk?" She rubbed his arm and squeezed his hand, gently pulling at it to get his attention.

"Yeah, I'm good. I mean, yeah, I'm a little messed up right now and feel like I could sleep for the next week, but… I'm good. Actually…" He pulled her in close by her waist and held her tightly, resting his chin on her head. "I think I got an idea for another movie."

He kissed the top of her head and she relaxed and leaned against him. She closed her eyes.

Nate closed his, too, as he played with the scenes for his next movie.

Made in the USA
Columbia, SC
06 February 2025

52332983R00057